a Letter to Harvey Milk

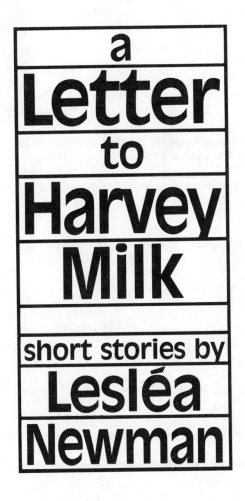

a Letter to Harvey Milk

short stories by Lesléa Newman

Firebrand
Books
Ithaca, New York

Part I of "The Best Revenge" first appeared under the title "Stalemate" in *Common Lives/Lesbian Lives*.

"A Letter To Harvey Milk" (formerly titled "Something To Pass The Time") was the Second Place Finalist in the 1987 Raymond Carver Short Story Contest.

"One *Shabbos* Evening" first appeared in *Conditions*.

Book and cover design by Mary A. Scott
Typesetting by Bets Ltd.

Printed on acid-free paper in the United States by McNaughton & Gunn

Library of Congress Cataloging-in-Publication Data

Newman, Lesléa.
    A letter to Harvey Milk.

        Contents: The gift—A letter to Harvey Milk—
Only a phase—[etc.]
        1. Lesbianism—Fiction.   2. Women, Jewish—Fiction.
I. Title.
PS3564.E91628L47   1988   813'.54   88-3923
ISBN 0-932379-44-3
ISBN 0-932379-43-5 (pbk.)

For My Grandmothers

Ida Newman (1902-1978)
aleha ha-sholom

Ruth Levin (1890-   )
kinehora

Acknowledgments

A very big thank you to the women who first read these stories and told me I was on the right track: Linda Dearstyne, Tryna Hope, Arachne Rachel, Marilyn Silberglied-Stewart, and Sarah Van Arsdale. I also thank Grace Paley for teaching me the art of listening to others, and Joan Larkin for teaching me the art of listening to myself. I am grateful to Rena Fisher, Rebecca Lillian, Kol, and the reference librarian at the Forbes Library in Northampton, Massachusetts for answering my endless questions, and to Cheryl Clarke for the fine editing work she did on "One *Shabbos* Evening." A special thank you to Nancy K. Bereano for her support and encouragement, Linda McRoy for her patience and understanding, and Couscous Kerouac for her inspiring company. And lastly, I am especially grateful, as always, to H.P. and all our mutual friends.

Contents

The Gift

To be a Jew in the twentieth century
Is to be offered a gift...
Muriel Rukeyser
"Letter To The Front"

Rachel is five years old. She is going out for a walk with her father. It is a windy day near the end of autumn, and Rachel is wearing her red wool coat with the real fur collar. Today is Sunday. Every Sunday Rachel's father takes her out on an adventure, so her mother can have a little peace and quiet. Sometimes they go to a diner for lunch, sometimes they go out for a little ice cream, and sometimes they just walk and walk through the streets of New York, with Rachel holding tightly to her father's hand.

Today they are walking through a part of Brooklyn that Rachel doesn't recognize. Her father stops to look at some books stacked high on a cart outside a bookshop. Rachel notices right away that these are grown-up books—not big and shiny like her picture books at home, but old and dusty. Her father picks one up to read. When he turns the pages, some of them crumble, and bits of them fall into the street and mix with the dry brown leaves whirling around their shoes.

Rachel's father picks up another book, holds it up close to his nose, and begins to read. He reads and reads and reads. Rachel is getting bored. She starts hopping up and down, first on one foot and then on the other. She wants to keep walking maybe, or just go home.

All of a sudden, Rachel notices a man coming toward them. He is short, not tall like her father, and he is wearing all black—black shoes, black pants, black coat, funny black hat. And swaying back and forth in the middle of all this black is the man's long white beard. Rachel gets more and more excited as the man draws near. She stops hopping up and down on her left foot and grabs her father's arm. "Daddy, Daddy," Rachel says, pulling at her father's sleeve with one hand and pointing with the other. "Is that Santa Claus? Why is he wearing those funny clothes?"

Rachel's father looks up from his book and sees the old Chasidic Jew coming toward them. He stares at the old man, and the old man stares at him. The old man moves slowly; Rachel's father's face does not move at all. Now Rachel is frightened. She watches the old man approach, and it is as if her father is watching himself in a mirror, growing older, until he looks just like the old man; and it is as if the old man is watching himself growing younger, until he looks just like her father. Then the old man passes them, and Rachel's father becomes young again. He puts the book back on the cart, reaches down for Rachel's hand, and they start their long walk home without a word.

Rachel is eight years old. She is standing in the kitchen with her back leaning against the counter, her arms folded across her chest, and her lower lip sticking way out. Rachel's mother is making soup, and Rachel is mad that her mother is paying more attention to the soup than to her.

"But why can't we have a Christmas tree?" Rachel asks again.

"Because Jews don't celebrate Christmas," her mother says, in a voice stretched so tight it sounds like it's going to break.

Rachel watches her mother's back, and her pout turns into a scowl. That's no reason, she thinks, staring down at the blue linoleum floor. I hate you, Rachel mouths silently, as her eyes travel across the floor and stop at her mother's feet. Rachel is so mad right now that she hates everything about her mother—her scuffy white slippers, her baggy stockings, her flowered housedress, her yellow apron, the *shmate* on her head, even the *knaydlach* she is rolling into a perfect ball between her two small hands.

Rachel tries once more. "How about a *Chanukah* bush then?"

"There's no such thing," her mother answers, turning around to face Rachel with the wooden spoon still in her hand. "Shush now, your father will be home soon. Do you want to pick out the candles?"

"No," Rachel says, and she stomps out of the kitchen to sit on the hallway steps. It is the seventh night of *Chanukah*, and she has saved all the red candles—her favorite color—for tonight. But now she even hates them. Rachel doesn't want to light the *menorah* and recite the blessing. She wants to sing "We Wish You A Merry Christmas," and she wants a tree. A tree, Rachel thinks, with tinsel and little colored balls and a string of popcorn hanging on it, and lots of presents underneath it, and pretty lights blinking on and off, and a beautiful angel on top. Like they have everywhere, Rachel thinks, with her chin on her fist, everywhere. At school, across the street at her best friend Kathy's house, even on TV. "Everywhere," Rachel whispers loudly, so her mother will hear. "Everywhere but here."

Rachel is ten years old. It is spring, and Rachel knows better than to ask her mother if the Easter bunny is coming to visit their house. Jews don't celebrate Easter, Jews celebrate *Pesach*, her mother has told her. Rachel doesn't like Passover very much. She doesn't get any presents, like at *Chanukah*, and she can't eat any of her favorite foods, like tuna fish sandwiches or vanilla ice-cream cones with jimmies or Sara Lee chocolate-frosted pound cake. Instead she has to carry peanut butter and jelly on *matzo* sandwiches to school while all the other kids get to bring pretty blue and pink and lavender hard-boiled eggs in their lunch boxes. Rachel's *matzo* sandwiches make her thirsty, and they're hard to eat. They get crumbly and make a big mess on the table and all over Rachel's lap.

Rachel is smart, though. She saves up all her milk money and by Friday she has fifteen cents, enough to buy a package of chocolate-chip cookies. She trades the cookies for half of Melanie Thompson's bologna and cheese sandwich. Right before she takes the first bite, Rachel looks around the lunchroom. She has a funny feeling in her stomach. What if God punishes her, or worse than that, what if her mother finds out? Rachel takes a bite, chews rapidly, and swallows. She looks around again. Everything seems normal. Billy McNamara is still shooting spitballs at Marlene DiBenedito, and Alice Johnson is still sitting all by herself, eating a banana with her nose in a book, pretending she doesn't care that nobody likes her. Lightning doesn't strike, and Rachel's mother doesn't rush in hysterically to snatch the forbidden food out of her daughter's hand.

Rachel finishes the sandwich, feeling relieved and a little disappointed at the same time.

Rachel is fourteen. She is getting taller. Her hips are getting wider. There is hair under her arms and between her legs, and now she has to wear a bra. She hooks it around her waist, swivels it around so that the cups are in front, and pulls the straps up onto her arms. Rachel misses her soft cotton undershirts. She keeps them at the bottom of her underwear drawer, and sometimes when she is alone in her room, she piles them on her lap and talks to them and cries.

Rachel is getting very pretty. Everyone says so: her mother, her father, her Aunt Esther, everyone except her grandmother. "*Oy,* such an ugly face you got. A face like a monkey," she says, pinching both of Rachel's cheeks. "What are we gonna do with such an ugly monkey face? Take her back to Macy's where we got her, that's what we're gonna do."

Rachel hates when her grandmother says that, though she likes to believe she was adopted. She also hates it when anyone says she is pretty. I'm not pretty, Rachel thinks, staring at herself in the mirror. I'm too short and too fat and my hair is too frizzy. Rachel wishes she was tall and thin and blonde, with hair the color of yellow crayons and eyes the color of the sky. She wants to look like the models in *Glamour* magazine. She wishes she would get taller, and her father offers to string her up on a rack. Very funny, she tells him. She wishes she would get thinner, and her mother tells her to go to Weight Watchers. Gross, Rachel says. But most of all, Rachel wishes her hair would be straight.

Every other night, Rachel washes her hair. First she shampoos it with Head and Shoulders and then she rinses it with Tame. She combs it out, and before she even steps into her bathrobe, the ends are already beginning to frizz. Rachel scoops up a gob of Dippity Doo and smoothes it onto her hair. She divides her hair into eight sections and wraps each one around a pink roller, big enough to put her fist through. Then she ties a net around her head and sits under the hair dryer for forty minutes, until her hair is dry and her ears are bright red.

Now Rachel parts her hair in the middle and brushes it out, checking her reflection in the mirror for ridges or bumps from the bobby pins. Before she goes to bed, she gathers all her hair up in a ponytail at the top of her head and wraps it around an empty orange juice can. Rachel sleeps on her stomach with her head hanging off the bed, and before she falls asleep she makes a deal with God: I'll be good, she whispers into the darkness, if you promise that tomorrow you won't make it rain.

Rachel is fifteen. She is going to the beach with her best friend Kathy. Kathy is tall and thin and blonde—everything Rachel would like to be. She even wears the perfect bathing suit: an itsy-bitsy pink bikini that Rachel would give her life to be able to fit into. Rachel wears a black one-piece suit she bought last week with her mother. Rachel hates going shopping with her mother. She always says things like, "I'm not buying you that. Your whole *tuchus* is sticking out," or, "Too bad, kid, you got those famous Goldstein hips." Try as she might, Rachel couldn't make her hips any smaller, no matter how little she ate or what diet she went on. She had to admit, though she hated to, that the Goldstein family had indeed left their mark.

I wish I looked like Kathy, Rachel thinks, as the sun warms her skin. She is lying on her back on a big blue beach towel, with her arms over her head so that her belly will look flatter. She squints into the sun and then looks behind her past her arms. There is a man lying a little ways away from them and he is wearing boxer trunks with nothing underneath. Rachel can see up his skinny hairy legs, to his thing, which rests inside his bathing suit against his left thigh. The man is sleeping, and his thing seems to be sleeping too. Rachel pokes Kathy on the shoulder.

"Look," she whispers, pointing with her eyes.

"Oh my God," Kathy whispers back, and they giggle and turn away and then look again.

When Rachel gets home from the beach, her mother is on the phone. "She's fine," she says, in a tone of voice that lets Rachel know her mother is talking about her. "She just got back from the beach and she's so dark, *vay iss mir*, she looks like a *shvartze*." Rachel doesn't know what a *shvartze* is, but from the way her mother says it, she knows it is something Jewish and not very good to look like. Rachel runs upstairs to consult the mirror, but she doesn't look like anything much, except herself.

Rachel is sixteen. She is sitting on the couch next to her father, looking at old photographs. The big album is spread across both their laps. Four black triangles, one in each corner, hold each picture in place, though some of them have gotten loose and stick together between the pages.

Rachel's father points to all the pictures and tells her who everyone is. "That's your Great-Aunt Yetta," he says, pointing. "That's your Uncle Mann. That's your Grandpa Harry, who died right before you were born."

"Who's this?" Rachel asks, staring at a photo of a young girl, about the same age that Rachel is now. She wears a white frilly dress and black shoes with thin ankle straps. Her father lifts the album up on his lap and bends down closer to the picture.

"Who is that?" he repeats softly to himself. "Oh for God's sake, that's your Aunt Esther with her old nose." Her father lowers the album and chuckles. "Look at that. God, that must be an old picture. Must be 1942, maybe '43." Now Rachel bends closer to see the picture. It doesn't look like Aunt Esther to her. The girl in the picture had her hands clasped tightly behind her back. She was wearing dark red lipstick, but she wasn't smiling.

"I didn't know Aunt Esther had a nose job," Rachel says to her father.

"Oh, sure she did. Both my sisters had one—your Aunt Selma and your cousin Robin, too. Thank God you got your mother's nose. Look, there's you at the old house on Avenue J. Do you remember that house?" He lowers his own nose closer to get a better look at the page.

Rachel is seventeen. She takes the train into the city with Kathy to visit the Museum of Modern Art. Rachel pretends to admire the paintings, though she really doesn't think they look all that different from the crayon drawings of her five-year-old cousin Nathan, which her Aunt Selma has hanging on her refrigerator door with magnets shaped like orange slices and banana peels.

Rachel and Kathy go into the gift shop to buy some postcards, and then Kathy says she has to go to the bathroom. Rachel stands by herself, slowly turning the creaky postcard rack.

"Hey *chica*, hey mama," a man's voice calls, and without turning around, Rachel knows he is talking to her. She ignores him, just like her mother taught her to, and stays right where she is, waiting for Kathy. The man comes right beside her and puts his hand on the postcard rack so it can't turn. He is wearing black pants and a brown corduroy coat, and he is short, about the same height as Rachel.

The man starts speaking to Rachel in Spanish. She shakes her head, holding up one hand. "Listen, I don't speak Spanish. I'm sorry," she says, and her voice is sorry, too, as if she has done something wrong.

But the man doesn't believe her. "C'mon. No kidding me. You speak Spanish, yes?" He smiles and Rachel notices he has bright white teeth.

"No, you don't understand. I'm not Spanish. I'm Jewish," Rachel says, backing up a little.

Now the man's smile grows even bigger, as though Rachel has made a joke. "No," he says. "You are no Jewish. You are too pretty for Jewish. You speak Spanish, yes?" The man leans toward Rachel, and now she feels afraid. She leaves the gift shop quickly and walks swiftly through the lobby toward the bathroom where, much to her relief, she sees Kathy's face floating in her direction above the crowd.

Rachel is eighteen. It is *Yom Kippur*, and today she does not go to school. She goes to services instead with her mother and father. Rachel puts on her new plaid skirt, her soft red sweater, and a pretty gold bracelet. Then she laces up her red high-topped sneakers and goes downstairs where her parents are waiting for her.

Her mother looks her up and down. When her eyes reach Rachel's feet, she starts to scream. "What's that on your feet? Get upstairs and put on your good shoes."

"But Ma, you're not supposed to wear leather today. You're supposed to give thanks to the animals. Even the Rabbi goes in sneakers." Rachel stares at her mother in defiance.

"Since when is she so religious?" Rachel's mother asks the ceiling. The ceiling offers no reply, and Rachel's mother turns back to her daughter. "I don't care if the Rabbi is going barefoot, you are not wearing those sneakers to *shul.* Now get upstairs and change your shoes. Do you hear me?''

Rachel hears her. She changes her shoes.

Rachel is still eighteen. She is going away to college. She has survived high school, much to her great relief and astonishment. She is in the back seat of the car with her pillow, two blankets, a suitcase, and a potted plant. The rest of her things are in the trunk, and her parents are in the front seat. They talk and talk while Rachel pretends to be asleep. They talk about the pretty New England towns they are driving through; they talk about where they will stop for lunch and how hungry they are and what they will eat; and they talk about Rachel and how big she is already going off to college.

They arrive at Rachel's college in the mid-afternoon. Rachel will be living in a suite with three other girls, and she is glad none of them are there yet. Rachel doesn't want anyone to meet her parents. She is embarrassed by how loud they talk and ashamed of her mother's shabby fake-leather coat.

Rachel's parents leave, and the three other girls arrive soon after dinner. Rachel sits on an overturned milk crate and watches them unpack. Their names are Debbie, Donna, and Marie. None of them are from New York. None of them are anything like Rachel. Soon they all sit in the bare living room, two on the orange couch and two on blue directors' chairs. They talk. Debbie tells them she grew up on a farm in Vermont, Donna says she comes from Illinois, and Marie is from Pennsylvania. Rachel tells them she is from New York, only the way she says it, it sounds more like New *Yawk,* and the other girls laugh at how she talks. Rachel vows to practice her *R*'s, and she doesn't hear what Donna is saying.

"Are you Jewish?'' Donna asks her again.

Rachel thinks for a minute. "No,'' she says slowly. "I used to be, but I'm not anymore.'' And suddenly Rachel is talking and laughing with her new friends and feeling free—free as a downy bird that has just pecked her way out of a baby blue egg with a beak as sharp and pointed as her Aunt Esther's new nose.

Rachel is nineteen-and-a-half. She has a boyfriend named Eddie. Rachel and Eddie are in bed together. It is 11:30 in the morning, and Eddie's roommate is at his biology class. After the class there is a lab, so he will be gone most of the day.

Eddie is smoking a cigarette. He leans back to grind the butt out in the ashtray on the floor. He has nothing on except a thin gold chain around his neck. Rachel is naked, too.

Eddie lazily stretches his arms over his head and grins at Rachel. "I'm starving." He brings one arm down to stroke her hair. "I wonder what delicious delicacies they're going to bestow upon us in the dining hall today?" he says, in a pseudo-intellectual voice.

"Probably spam sandwiches and jello mold with floating fruit cocktail," Rachel answers, wrinkling up her nose.

"Hey, what's the difference between a Jewish American Princess and a bowl of jello?" Eddie asks. Rachel doesn't answer. "One moves when you eat it and the other doesn't," he says, diving under the blankets. Rachel opens her legs wide and hugs Eddie's head with her thighs. I'll show him a thing or two, Rachel thinks, as Eddie emerges from the blankets, pulls her close and slides inside her. Rachel knows what is expected of her. She digs her nails into Eddie's back and moves for all she is worth.

Rachel is twenty years old. Her dorm is having a Christmas party, and this year she is Donna's Secret Santa. She goes downtown to buy a little present to leave outside Donna's door. The trees that line Main Street are decorated with red and green lights that blink on and off, and the sidewalk is filled with people rushing about with packages of toys and wrapping paper grasped tightly in their hands.

Rachel turns down a side street where it is quieter and enters a store. The store is filled with Indian clothing made of 100 percent cotton, costume jewelry, cards, posters, and knickknacks. An old man and woman sit behind the counter, eating. Rachel walks around touching a mauve skirt, inspecting a wooden elephant, picking up a pair of white cloth shoes. She walks over to the jewelry counter and looks at a row of silver earrings.

"For something special you're looking maybe?"

Rachel raises her head and looks at the old man who has spoken to her. He wears a *yarmulke* on his head, and the old woman next to him has a silver *chai* around her neck. They are sitting on little wooden stools with napkins on their laps, eating potato pancakes out of a plastic container between them. Rachel stares at the food.

"You want a *latke* maybe?" the woman asks, smiling at Rachel and holding out a pancake.

"No thanks," Rachel stammers, aware now that she has been staring. "I just came in for a *tchotchke*." The Yiddish word, coming from nowhere, flies out of Rachel's mouth.

"*Tchotchkes* she wants? *Oy*, do we got *tchotchkes*," the man says, coming out from behind the counter. "Little animals we got, and wooden baskets, paper fans maybe you like?" He gives Rachel a guided tour of his shop, and she picks out a hand-painted wooden giraffe.

Rachel pays the man and sees that now the old woman is eating some applesauce out of a jar with a plastic spoon. "Take, take a *latke* home, you'll have it for later," she says, handing Rachel a package wrapped in tin foil. Rachel picks up the *latke* and Donna's present and leaves the store.

When she gets back to the dorm, Rachel hides Donna's present under her bed and takes off her coat, hat, and scarf. She goes into the bathroom with the bundle of tin foil and locks the door. The old woman has given Rachel not one, but three potato pancakes. Rachel eats the *latkes* ravenously, then licks her fingers greedily, searching the tin foil for any stray crumbs she may have left behind.

Rachel is twenty-one. This is her last semester of college. She has learned a lot of things over the past three-and-a-half years. She has learned about Art History and Abnormal Psychology and American Literature Since 1945. She has learned about drinking sombreros and singapore slings, smoking pot, and taking speed. But the most important thing she's learned is that she likes women better than she likes men.

Rachel has a girlfriend. Her name is Angie. They do everything together. They eat meals together in the big dining hall, they study together on the top floor of the library, and they sleep together in Angie's tiny single room.

One Saturday, Rachel and Angie get dressed all in purple and walk downtown holding hands. It is Gay Pride Day, and this is the first year there is going to be a parade in their town. They stand in a school yard with about 300 people, and there are balloons, dogs wearing bandannas around their necks and chasing frisbees, even a marching band with a man and a woman baton twirler.

Now the march begins. Rachel and Angie get on line and start up the street. They feel very happy stepping to the beat of the drums. They walk up Main Street proudly, past all the little shops and restaurants they have gone into together many times before. People line the streets. Some raise their fists and cheer; other simply stand there staring.

At the top of Main Street the march takes a turn into a park. At one side of the park entrance stands a small group of people holding signs that say, *God made Adam and Eve, NOT Adam and Steve*, and *Jesus loves the sinner but not the sin*. On the other side of the park two girls are standing with a big sign made out of an old white sheet stretched between them. Their sign says, *NEVER AGAIN*, and it is decorated with women's symbols, men's symbols, and Jewish stars. Rachel looks at the sign and feels tears welling up in her eyes and flowing down her cheeks. She turns her face away so Angie won't see, and wipes her eyes with the back of her sleeve.

Rachel is twenty-two. She and Angie live in an apartment in town. Angie is in graduate school, and Rachel is working in an office and daydreaming about becoming a famous movie star or winning the lottery and getting at least a million dollars.

Rachel is grouchy when she comes home. She doesn't like working in an office and she doesn't get to spend enough time with Angie. She's always at a meeting, or studying at the library. Rachel eats dinner by herself, listening to the radio. The news is on. Otto Frank, Anne Frank's father, has died today in Switzerland, at the age of ninety-one. Rachel puts down her fork. *The Diary of Anne Frank* was one of her favorite books when she was a little girl. She walks over to the bookshelf to see if she still has it. She does. Rachel takes it down and begins to read. She gets so absorbed in the book that she crawls into bed at 10:00 with all her clothes on, still reading. Angie comes in at 11:00 and finds Rachel asleep, with the book on the bed upside down beside her.

"Hi, honey," Angie whispers, kissing Rachel awake. She slips into bed beside her and gathers her up in her arms. "I missed you all day," Angie says, kissing Rachel's warm cheek. "Hey, you still have all your clothes on. Let me undress you." Angie unbuttons Rachel's shirt and plants little kisses all across her chest. Soon her mouth finds Rachel's breast. Rachel cradles Angie's head in her arms and before long, they are rocking each other gently and moaning together softly.

"You feel so good," Rachel murmurs, as Angie unbuttons her pants and slides them down around Rachel's feet. Angie touches Rachel in the way Rachel likes best, and just as she starts to come, Rachel bursts into tears.

"What is it, baby? What is it?" Angie holds her as she sobs and sobs. "Never again," Rachel cries out, sniffling and gasping for air. "Never again," she repeats, crying uncontrollably now. Angie is puzzled, but she holds Rachel, stroking her hair and murmuring, "It's all right, Rachel. It's all right."

Suddenly, Rachel is furious with Angie. "It's not all right," she says sharply, pulling herself away. "What if they came tomorrow? What if they're coming right now? Would you hide me? Would you?"

"Who, Rachel? Who's coming to get you?"

"The Nazis," Rachel says, a fresh batch of tears falling from her eyes.

"Oh, Rachel, that's over. You're safe now. No one's coming to get you."

"What if they are? What if they're coming right now? Where would I go? Who would take care of me?"

"I would, honey. I would hide you. Of course I would. Rachel, I won't let anyone take you away from me. I'll hold on to you really tight, just like this." Rachel lets Angie encircle her in her warm arms, even though she doesn't believe her.

Rachel is twenty-three. It is April, and she has been invited to two feminist *seders*. She stands in the kitchen looking at the *Women For Peace* calendar hanging on the wall. Angie is sitting at the table drinking lemon grass tea.

"We can go to Amy's *seder* Thursday night and Meryl's on Friday, O.K.?" Rachel asks.

Angie pours some honey into her tea. "Do we have to go to both?" she asks. "I'm getting a little Jew-ed out."

"What?" Rachel's body jerks itself forward. This is the woman who touches me in all my secret places, Rachel thinks. This is the woman I'm going to spend the rest of my life with. "What did you say?" Rachel asks, sitting down next to Angie at the table.

"Never mind," Angie says, letting out a deep sigh. "You have *seders* for Passover, right, and the *menorah* is for *Chanukah?*"

"Right," Rachel says, leaning back in her chair. "And let's see. You have a tree for Christmas and a rabbit for Easter, and you put *shmutz* on your forehead for Ash Wednesday and you give up something for Lent on Good Friday, and . . . ."

"O.K., O.K., I was only trying. You don't have to get nasty," Angie says, staring out the window, the sky reflected in her blue eyes.

"Sorry," Rachel mutters, but she doesn't really mean it. She's sorry Angie hurt her, and she's glad she hurt her back.

Rachel is twenty-four. She and Angie aren't girlfriends anymore. It is December, and Rachel is out doing errands. She goes to the post office and asks for five stamps. The clerk hands her a strip of stamps, three with pictures of Christmas trees and two with a child's drawing of Santa Claus.

"I don't want these," Rachel says, handing them back. The clerk gives her five stamps with American flags. Rachel isn't crazy about these either, but they'll have to do. She pays the postal clerk and waits for her change. The clerk hands her some coins and says, "Merry Christmas."

"I don't celebrate Christmas. I'm Jewish," Rachel says, as she drops the money into her wallet.

"Oh, I'm sorry," the woman says, and Rachel can tell by her voice that she's not sorry for the mistake she's made, but rather for Rachel's misfortune. "Well, have a happy holiday then."

I'm not having a holiday, Rachel thinks, as she shoves her wallet into her coat pocket. *Chanukah* was over five days ago. She leaves the post office wrapped in a cloud of angry silence.

Rachel is twenty-five. She has a new girlfriend named Bernie. Bernie's real name is Bernice and she is Jewish. Rachel is going shopping for Bernie's *Chanukah* presents. She is going to get her eight presents—seven little ones and one big one.

Rachel walks around town and finds her way to the women's bookstore that just opened several weeks ago. She's sure she'll be able to find something there. At the front of the store there is a bulletin board with lots of buttons, and Rachel thinks maybe she can find something funny for Bernie. Her eyes search the little shiny circles until she finds the perfect one: *This Butch Melts*. Rachel reaches up to get the button, and her eyes follow the motion of her hand, until they rest on another button: *I Survived A Jewish Mother*.

Rachel looks away, then looks at the button again. *I Survived Kent State*, she thinks. *I Survived Three Mile Island*. But *I Survived A Jewish Mother*? Rachel takes the button down and brings it over to the cash register. The woman behind the counter looks up from the invoice she is checking.

"This button really offends me," Rachel says, with her heart pounding against her chest. The woman looks down at the button, then up at Rachel's face. "I'm Jewish, too," the woman says. So what? Rachel thinks. She says nothing. "Those buttons are made by a feminist company," the woman says, as if that explains even more. Rachel waits, but the woman says nothing else. Rachel asks, "How many of them do you have?"

The woman opens a wooden drawer and fishes around among buttons, key chains, and loose coins. She counts out eight buttons. "I'll take them all," Rachel says, handing the woman a ten dollar bill. Her heart is still racing. Rachel puts her change in her wallet and her wallet into her shoulder bag. Then she reaches into her bag again, removes a felt-tipped pen, and uncaps it. She scribbles on all the buttons and asks the woman behind the counter if she has a trash can.

"Get out of my store," the woman says. Rachel and her beating heart leave.

Rachel is still twenty-five. She is going shopping for *Chanukah* candles. She gets in her car and drives to Waldbaum's. She asks the man in the courtesy booth where the *Chanukah* candles are. "Aisle six," he says. "International foods."

Rachel is a little wary as she walks toward aisle six. That man is the same one who told her last spring that the *matzo* was in the frozen food section, confusing *matzos* with bagels.

Rachel turns down aisle six, and her eyes scan the shelves until she comes to the Jewish food: *borsht*, applesauce, chicken soup in jars, potato pancake mix, *Shabbos* candles, *Yahrzeit* candles, but no *Chanukah* candles. Rachel walks up the aisle until she sees a man in a red smock pricing boxes of fortune cookies.

"Excuse me," Rachel says, "but I can't find the *Chanukah* candles." She walks back up the aisle with the man following behind her. The man looks up and down the shelves and points to the *Shabbos* candles. "There," he says.

"No, those are *Shabbos* candles. I want *Chanukah* candles."

The man studies the shelf and picks up a *Yahrzeit* candle. "Is this what you want?"

"No. I'm looking for a box of forty-four candles, all different colors, little, to fit into a *menorah*," Rachel says.

"A what?" The man puts the *Yahrzeit* candle back and picks up a box of *Shabbos* candles. "Look, these are very nice candles. Seventy-two in a box. Can't you make do?"

"Never mind," Rachel says, and she leaves the store. How can Waldbaum's not have *Chanukah* candles, she wonders, as she backs out of her parking space and heads for another store. It is the same at Stop and Shop, Price Chopper, the Food Co-op, and Store 24. By the time Rachel gets home, she is exhausted. She calls the synagogue, and the woman who answers the phone tells her she can buy candles at the Goodman Pharmacy on Grove Avenue. Rachel hangs up the phone and cries for an hour.

The next night is *Chanukah*. Bernie is coming over for dinner. Rachel gets home from work early and chops up apples for applesauce and grates potatoes for *latkes*. She is very happy, bustling about the kitchen and listening to *Fiddler On The Roof* on the stereo.

Bernie comes over at seven. She is tired, she has had a hard day at work. Her head hurts. She asks Rachel to turn down the music. She tells Rachel she isn't very hungry. Rachel is disappointed. At least they light the candles together.

Then Bernie tells Rachel she can't stay very long. She's going to a Christmas party at Mary Ann's house.

"A Christmas party!" Rachel says in astonishment. "On the first night of *Chanukah*? I thought we were spending the first night of *Chanukah* together."

Bernie thrusts her hands in her pockets and shifts her weight. "Well, I forgot Mary Ann's party was tonight, and I promised I would come weeks ago. Besides, I didn't know the first night was such a big deal. *Chanukah*'s eight nights. We can spend another night of it together."

"But this is the *first* night. Of course it's important." Rachel starts to whine. "And I made a whole dinner for you."

Bernie looks at the food on the stove. "Well, I don't like *latkes* so much anyway. They're too greasy," she says. "Look, why don't you come with me to Mary Ann's? I just have to stop at my house and get her present."

"You bought her a Christmas present?" Rachel is practically yelling now.

"Well, yeah." Bernie thrusts her hands deeper into her pockets and fingers her change.

"But Bernie, you're Jewish!"

"I know I'm Jewish."

"Then how come you're buying someone a Christmas present?"

"Mary Ann's not *someone*. She's my best friend."

"So, did she buy you a *Chanukah* present?" Rachel asks, leaning her back against the sink and folding her arms.

"No." Bernie stares down at Rachel's feet.

"Then why did you buy her a Christmas present? And why are you going off to celebrate her holiday with her instead of staying here to celebrate our holiday with me?"

"What's wrong with doing something special for a friend that you love?" Now Bernie is yelling, too.

"Then why doesn't she do something special for you and buy you a present for *Chanukah*?"

"Because she's not Jewish."

"And you're not Catholic."

"Rachel." Bernie lets out a deep sigh. "Christmas isn't a Catholic holiday anymore. It's a universal holiday."

"That's bullshit."

"Rachel," Bernie sighs again, "do you really think Mary Ann is celebrating the birth of Jesus Christ?"

"Yes."

"Well, she isn't." Bernie is pacing around the kitchen floor. She stops in front of Rachel. "She just likes having a tree and a party because Christmas was the best day of her lousy childhood every year and. . ."

"Well, it was the worst day of mine," Rachel yells, flinging up her hands. "Go then. Have a great time. Kiss someone under the mistletoe for me."

"I will," Bernie yells into the night, as she yanks open the door. Rachel closes it behind her and sits down to eat the *latkes* by herself, salty tears running down her cheeks.

Rachel is twenty-six. She needs some new clothes. She goes downtown to a used clothing store called Clothes Encounters and begins to browse. Usually Rachel finds something she likes at Clothes Encounters, but not today. On her way out she stops at the $.50 bin to look at some scarves. She squats down and rummages around. Her eye falls on something white and shiny, trimmed with blue. It is a *tallis*. Rachel can't believe it. She rubs the shiny material against her face. How did it ever wind up here, she wonders. Rachel pays for the *tallis* and brings it home. She sits in her rocking chair, braiding the strands of the *tallis* together, just like she did when she was a little girl sitting next to her father in *shul*. Rachel is lonely. She and Bernie aren't girlfriends anymore. Rachel wants a new lover. Being a lesbian is lonely, Rachel thinks. Being a Jew is lonely. Being alive is lonely, she reminds herself. A tear slips down her cheek, and Rachel wipes it with the corner of the *tallis*.

Rachel decides to call a friend, but her line is busy. She calls someone else and gets an answering machine. Rachel takes a warm bath and drinks some camomile tea. She sleeps with the *tallis* under her pillow, one hand stroking the shiny cloth the same way she would pet the shiny part of her baby blanket to put herself to sleep twenty-five years ago.

Rachel is twenty-eight. She has just moved in with her girlfriend Nina. Rachel loves Nina very much, and Nina seems to love Rachel. Nina is not Jewish, but she knows some things about Judaism, like why the Jews were driven out of Egypt and who Miriam the Prophet was and how you're supposed to kiss the *mezuzah* when you go in and out of the front door.

Nina tells Rachel that even though she can't be Jewish for her, she can be supportive. She says maybe she'll take a Hebrew class or a Jewish history class. Rachel doesn't like that idea. She doesn't want Nina to know more about being Jewish than she does. She tells Nina so, and Nina gives her a big hug. "It's O.K., Rachel," she says. "I won't if you don't want me to. But it would be neat to know Hebrew so I could go to temple with you."

Rachel doesn't tell Nina she hasn't been to *shul* in ten years. Today they are going to an all-day lesbian conference. There are lots of workshops and activities to choose from. Rachel decides to go to a writing workshop in the morning, and a cross-cultural relationship workshop with Nina in the afternoon.

Rachel enjoys the writing workshop. The workshop leader is very encouraging and supportive and full of good ideas. The women write for half an hour and then go around the room sharing their work. Rachel is very moved by the words that the other women read.

As they go around, a few women decide not to share their writing. The leader says that's O.K., there's no pressure. One woman apologizes. The workshop leader says, "It's really all right. Nobody's going to force you to do anything you don't want to here. This isn't a Nazi concentration camp."

Rachel is stunned. She looks around at the faces of the women in the circle, all of them paying rapt attention to a woman in a green jumpsuit who is reading a poem about her grandmother. Rachel slowly scans the room. I am the only Jew here, she thinks, as the tears begin to rise.

After the workshop, Rachel approaches the teacher. Her heart is beating in her throat. "What you said," she says, faltering, looking down at her hands. . . this is a famous writer, Rachel reminds herself. "What you said," she begins again, "about this workshop not being like a concentration camp," she pauses again and then bursts out, "How can you compare not sharing your writing with being in a Nazi camp? Do you have any idea what went on there? This is nothing," Rachel says, gesturing with one hand around the room. "Nothing," she repeats.

The workshop leader is very sorry. She apologizes a hundred times. She supports Rachel. She says she's glad Rachel brought it up and tells her she is brave.

Rachel doesn't feel brave. She feels tired and a little apprehensive about the next workshop. She and Nina go to Room 307 and sit down. There are already about fifteen women there. The leader of the workshop smiles. She is a white woman.

"Welcome to this workshop on interracial relationships," she says. Rachel and Nina look at each other. "I thought it was cross-cultural relationships," Nina whispers. "It must have gotten changed," Rachel whispers back. "Should we stay?" Nina asks her. Rachel shrugs her shoulders. "I guess so," she says.

The workshop leader has the group break off into pairs and talk about the first time they met somebody from a different racial group and what that was like. Then they talk about an interracial relationship they are having right now and what they're learning from it. Then they talk about what barriers prevent them from having more interracial relationships.

After the third question, the women regroup in a circle for discussion. Rachel smiles at Nina when she comes back to sit next to her. They listen to the discussion. A white woman talks about how difficult her parents make it when she brings her Black lover home for a visit. Another white woman raises her hand. She tells the group that she is involved with a Jewish woman, and that her lover's parents are Holocaust survivors.

"It's really hard to be around them," the woman says, "especially when they act in that stereotypically obnoxious Jewish way."

Rachel's body stiffens for the second time that day. She looks around this group of faces, asking herself again, *Am I the only Jew in the room? Does anybody else have ears?* Now everyone is listening to a Black woman who is speaking. Rachel is afraid to look at Nina. She sits in silence until the workshop is almost over. When there are only about five minutes left, she rises slowly and walks to the front of the room to stand next to the workshop leader. The woman turns. "Yes?" she asks, putting her hand on Rachel's shoulder, and Rachel bursts into tears.

Rachel is twenty-nine. It is *Rosh Hashanah*. She stays home from work to go to *shul*. Nina offers to come with her, but Rachel says no, this is something she needs to do by herself. Nina says, "Good *yontif*," the way Rachel has taught her, and kisses her cheek. Rachel tells her that later they will eat apples and honey together so the new year will be sweet. Nina tells Rachel she has a little present for her. "Do you want it now or later?" she asks. "Later," Rachel says. "I don't want to be late for *shul*."

Nina leaves for work, and Rachel gets dressed. She puts on black pants, a fuzzy white sweater, and a pair of turquoise earrings. She laces up her red high-topped sneakers and wears a labyris and a Jewish star around her neck. She buttons her coat, thrusts her hands in her pockets, and starts the long walk to shul.

As Rachel walks, she thinks about all the things that have happened to her over the years. She thinks about being a little girl who wanted a Christmas tree more than anything in the whole world. She thinks about how ashamed she was to take peanut butter and *matzo* sandwiches to school, and all the years she spent trying to diet and straighten her hair. Rachel walks quickly through the streets of her town, not paying much attention to the cars that pass her, all the while thinking. She thinks about marching with Angie in the Gay Pride March and about fighting with Bernie about Christmas. And she thinks a lot about Nina; how she offered to go to *shul* with her that morning and how sometimes she asks Rachel to sing her to sleep. "Sing me a Hebrew song," she says to her. "Your voice sounds so beautiful when you sing in Hebrew."

Rachel walks and walks. Tucked under her arm is her *tallis* in a little blue velvet bag she has sewn herself. She wonders what her mother would think to see her daughter carrying a *tallis*. Rachel remembers how happy her mother was last year to receive a New Year's card from her. The card had a picture of a woman with a shawl on her head, chopping apples in her kitchen, and Rachel had written inside, "Thank you for never letting me forget who I am."

Rachel also remembers her first day of college when she told her three roommates that she wasn't a Jew and how she hadn't said anything to Eddie whenever he told his awful Jewish American Princess jokes. Rachel is thinking about all of these things as she turns onto Elmwood Avenue and the synagogue comes into view. She notices a young couple across the street and smiles at them, knowing where they are going. The young woman calls to her son not to run so fast and to wait for his father before he crosses the street.

Rachel enters the *shul* and takes a prayer book from the shelf in the lobby. She is too shy to put on her *tallis*. She goes inside and sits down, holding the prayer book and the *tallis* on her lap. The Rabbi is reading in Hebrew. Rachel looks around to see if she can find anyone she knows. Her friend Aviva is sitting two rows in front of her, with a bunch of women Rachel doesn't know. One of the women is wearing a *yarmulke* on her head. When the Ark is open, Rachel tiptoes down the aisle and squeezes in next to Aviva. Aviva smiles. She is happy to see Rachel here. Aviva is wearing a grey sweater and a black skirt with little grey elf boots. She has a gold labyris with a Jewish star cut out of one of its blades around her neck.

The Rabbi begins to sing and the congregation sings with him. Rachel sees that Aviva can read Hebrew. She is moving her finger right to left across the page. Her voice is loud, strong and beautiful. Rachel cannot read Hebrew but she sings along, surprised that she remembers all the words and all the tunes. Rachel feels like a little girl again, and she half expects to see her mother and father sitting in front of her in the next aisle.

The Rabbi and the Cantor sing the *Shema* in loud, clear voices, and Rachel feels her heart swelling inside her chest. She repeats the *Shema* along with Aviva and the hundred or so other people in the small synagogue, letting the tears run down her cheeks like rain. Aviva turns to face Rachel, and Rachel does not turn away. They smile at each other, and Aviva squeezes Rachel's hand. She understands. Rachel has come home.

A Letter To Harvey Milk

for Harvey Milk 1930-1978

I.

The teacher says we should write about our life, everything that happened today. So *nu*, what's there to tell? Why should today be different than any other day? May 5, 1986. I get up, I have myself a coffee, a little cottage cheese, half an English muffin. I get dressed. I straighten up the house a little, nobody should drop by and see I'm such a slob. I go down to the Senior Center and see what's doing. I play a little cards, I have some lunch, a bagel with cheese. I read a sign in the cafeteria, Writing Class 2:00. I think to myself, why not, something to pass the time. So at two o'clock I go in. The teacher says we should write about our life.

Listen, I want to say to this teacher, I.B. Singer I'm not. You think anybody cares what I did all day? Even my own children, may they live and be well, don't call. You think the whole world is waiting to see what Harry Weinberg had for breakfast?

The teacher is young and nice. She says everybody has something important to say. Yeah, sure, when you're young you believe things like that. She has short brown hair and big eyes, a nice figure, *zaftig* like my poor Fannie, may she rest in peace. She's wearing a Star of David around her neck, hanging from a purple string, that's nice. She gave us all notebooks and told us we're gonna write something every day, and if we want we can even write at home. Who'd a thunk it, me—Harry Weinberg, seventy-seven-years old—scribbling in a notebook like a schoolgirl. Why not, it passes the time.

32

So after the class I go to the store, I pick myself up a little orange juice, a few bagels, a nice piece of chicken, I shouldn't starve to death. I go up, I put on my slippers, I eat the chicken, I watch a little TV, I write in this notebook, I get ready for bed. *Nu*, for this somebody should give me a Pulitzer Prize?

II.

Today the teacher tells us something about herself. She's a Jew, this we know from the *Mogen David* she wears around her neck. She tells us she wants to collect stories from old Jewish people, to preserve our history. *Oy*, such stories that I could tell her, shouldn't be preserved by nobody. She tells us she's learning Yiddish. For what, I wonder. I can't figure this teacher out. She's young, she's pretty, she shouldn't be with the old people so much. I wonder is she married. She doesn't wear a ring. Her grandparents won't tell her stories, she says, and she's worried that the Jews her age won't know nothing about the culture, about life in the *shtetls*. Believe me, life in the *shtetl* is nothing worth knowing about. Hunger and more hunger. Better off we're here in America, the past is past.

Then she gives us our homework, the homework we write in the class, it's a little *meshugeh*, but alright. She wants us to write a letter to somebody from our past, somebody who's no longer with us. She reads us a letter a child wrote to Abraham Lincoln, like an example. Right away I see everybody's getting nervous. So I raise my hand. "Teacher," I say, "you can tell me maybe how to address such a letter? There's a few things I've wanted to ask my wife for a long time." Everybody laughs. Then they start to write.

I sit for a few minutes, thinking about Fannie, thinking about my sister Frieda, my mother, my father, may they all rest in peace. But it's the strangest thing, the one I really want to write to is Harvey.

Dear Harvey:

You had to go get yourself killed for being a *faygeleh*? You couldn't let somebody else have such a great honor? Alright, alright, so you liked the boys, I wasn't wild about the idea. But I got used to it. I never said you wasn't welcome in my house, did I?

Nu, Harvey, you couldn't leave well enough alone? You had your own camera store, your own business, what's bad? You couldn't keep still about the boys, you weren't satisfied until the whole world knew? Harvey Milk, with the big ears and the big ideas, had to go make himself something, a big politician. I know, I know, I said, "Harvey, make something of yourself, don't be an old *shmegeggie* like me, Harry the butcher." So now I'm eating my words, and they stick like a chicken bone in my old throat.

It's a rotten world, Harvey, and rottener still without you in it. You know what happened to that *momzer*, Dan White? They let him out of jail, and he goes and kills himself so nobody else should have the pleasure. Now you know me, Harvey, I'm not a violent man. But this was too much, even for me. In the old country, I saw things you shouldn't know from, things you couldn't imagine one person could do to another. But here in America, a man climbs through the window, kills the Mayor of San Francisco, kills Harvey Milk, and a couple years later he's walking around on the street? This I never thought I'd see in my whole life. But from a country that kills the Rosenbergs, I should expect something different?

Harvey, you should be glad you weren't around for the trial. I read about it in the papers. The lawyer, that son of a bitch, said Dan White ate too many Twinkies the night before he killed you, so his brain wasn't working right. Twinkies, *nu*, I ask you. My kids ate Twinkies when they were little, did they grow up to be murderers, God forbid? And now, do they take the Twinkies down from the shelf, somebody else shouldn't go a little crazy, climb through a window, and shoot somebody? No, they leave them right there next to the cupcakes and the donuts, to torture me every time I go to the store to pick up a few things, I shouldn't starve to death.

Harvey, I think I'm losing my mind. You know what I do every week? Every week I go to the store, I buy a bag of jellybeans for you, you should have something to *nosh* on, I remember what a sweet tooth you have. I put them in a jar on the table, in case you should come in with another crazy petition for me to sign. Sometimes I think you're gonna just walk through my door and tell me it was another *meshugeh* publicity stunt.

Harvey, now I'm gonna tell you something. The night you died the whole city of San Francisco cried for you. Thirty thousand people marched in the street, I saw it on TV. Me, I didn't go down. I'm an old man, I don't walk so good, they said there might be riots. But no, there were no riots. Just people walking in the street, quiet, each one with a candle, until the street looked like the sky all lit up with a million stars. Old people, young people, Black people, white people, Chinese people. You name it, they were there. I remember thinking, Harvey must be so proud, and then I remembered you were dead and such a lump rose in my throat, like a grapefruit it was, and then the tears ran down my face like rain. Can you imagine, Harvey, an old man like me, sitting alone in his apartment, crying and carrying on like a baby? But it's the God's truth. Never did I carry on so in all my life.

And then all of a sudden I got mad. I yelled at the people on TV: for getting shot you made him into such a hero? You couldn't march for him when he was alive, he couldn't *shep* a little *naches*?

But *nu*, what good does getting mad do, it only makes my pressure go up. So I took myself a pill, calmed myself down.

Then they made speeches for you, Harvey. The same people who called you a *shmuck* when you were alive, now you were dead, they were calling you a *mensh*. You were a *mensh*, Harvey, a *mensh* with a heart of gold. You were too good for this rotten world. They just weren't ready for you.

Oy Harveleh, alav ha-sholom,
Harry

III.

Today the teacher asks me to stay for a minute after class. *Oy*, what did I do wrong now, I wonder. Maybe she didn't like my letter to Harvey? Who knows?

After the class she comes and sits down next to me. She's wearing purple pants and a white T-shirt. "*Feh*," I can just hear Fannie say. "God forbid she should wear a skirt? Show off her figure a little? The girls today dressing like boys and the boys dressing like girls—this I don't understand."

"Mr. Weinberg," the teacher says.

"Call me Harry," I says.

"O.K., Harry," she says. "I really liked the letter you wrote to Harvey Milk. It was terrific, really. It meant a lot to me. It even made me cry."

I can't even believe my own ears. My letter to Harvey Milk made the teacher cry?

"You see, Harry," she says, "I'm gay, too. And there aren't many Jewish people your age that are so open-minded. At least that I know. So your letter gave me lots of hope. In fact, I was wondering if you'd consider publishing it."

Publishing my letter? Again I couldn't believe my own ears. Who would want to read a letter from Harry Weinberg to Harvey Milk? No, I tell her. I'm too old for fame and glory. I like the writing class, it passes the time. But what I write is my own business. The teacher looks sad for a moment, like a cloud passes over her eyes. Then she says, "Tell me about Harvey Milk. How did you meet him? What was he like?" *Nu*, Harvey, you were a pain in the ass when you were alive, you're still a pain in the ass now that you're dead. Everybody wants to hear about Harvey.

So I tell her. I tell her how I came into the camera shop one day with a roll of film from when I went to visit the grandchildren. How we started talking, and I said, "Milk, that's not such a common name. Are you related to the Milks in Woodmere?" And so we found out we were practically neighbors forty years ago, when the children were young, before we moved out here. Gracie was almost the same age as Harvey, a couple years older, maybe, but they went to different schools. Still, Harvey leans across the counter and gives me such a hug, like I'm his own father.

I tell her more about Harvey, how he didn't believe there was a good *kosher* butcher in San Francisco, how he came to my store just to see. But all the time I'm talking I'm thinking to myself, no, it can't be true. Such a gorgeous girl like this goes with the girls, not with the boys? Such a *shanda*. Didn't God in His wisdom make a girl a girl and a boy a boy—boom they should meet, boom they should get married, boom they should have babies, and that's the way it is? Harvey I loved like my own son, but this I never could understand. And *nu*, why was the teacher telling me this, it's my business who she sleeps with? She has some sadness in her eyes, this teacher. Believe me I've known such sadness in my life, I can recognize it a hundred miles away. Maybe she's lonely. Maybe after class one day I'll take her out for a coffee, we'll talk a little bit, I'll find out.

IV.

It's 3:00 in the morning, I can't sleep. So *nu*, here I am with this crazy notebook. Who am I kidding, maybe I think I'm Yitzhak Peretz? What would the children think, to see their old father sitting up in his bathrobe with a cup of tea, scribbling in his notebook? *Oy, meyn kinder*, they should only live and be well and call their old father once in a while.

Fannie used to keep up with them. She could be such a *nudge*, my Fannie. "What's the matter, you're too good to call your old mother once in a while?" she'd yell into the phone. Then there'd be a pause. "Busy-shmusy," she'd yell even louder. "Was I too busy to change your diapers? Was I too busy to put food into your mouth?" *Oy*, I haven't got the strength, but Fannie could she yell and carry on.

You know sometimes, in the middle of the night, I'll reach across the bed for Fannie's hand. Without even thinking, like my hand got a mind of its own, it creeps across the bed, looking for Fannie's hand. After all this time, fourteen years she's been dead, but still, a man gets used to a few things. Forty-two years, the body doesn't forget. And my little *Faigl* had such hands, little *hentelehs*, tiny like a child's. But strong. Strong from kneading *challah*, from scrubbing clothes, from rubbing the children's backs to put them to sleep. My Fannie, she was so ashamed from those hands. After thirty-five years of marriage when finally, I could afford to buy her a diamond ring, she said no. She said it was too late already, she'd be ashamed. A girl needs nice hands to show off a diamond, her hands were already ruined, better yet buy a new stove.

Ruined? *Feh*. To me her hands were beautiful. Small, with veins running through them like rivers, and cracks in the skin like the desert. A hundred times I've kicked myself for not buying Fannie that ring.

V.

Today in the writing class the teacher read my notebook. Then she says I should make a poem about Fannie. "A poem," I says to her, "now Shakespeare you want I should be?" She says I have a good eye for detail. I says to her, "Excuse me Teacher, you live with a woman for forty-two years, you start to notice a few things."

She helps me. We do it together, we write a poem called "Fannie's Hands":

> Fannie's hands are two little birds
> that fly into her lap.
> Her veins are like rivers.
> Her skin is cracked like the desert.
> Her strong little hands
> baked *challah*, scrubbed clothes,
> rubbed the children's backs.
> Her strong little hands
> and my big clumsy hands
> fit together in the night
> like pieces of a jigsaw puzzle
> made in Heaven, by God.

So *nu*, who says you can't teach an old dog new tricks? I read it to the class and such a fuss they made. "A regular Romeo," one of them says. "If only my husband, may he live and be well, would write such a poem for me," says another. I wish Fannie was still alive, I could read it to her. Even the teacher was happy, I could tell, but still, there was a ring of sadness around her eyes.

After the class I waited till everybody left, they shouldn't get the wrong idea, and I asked the teacher would she like to go get a coffee. "*Nu*, it's enough writing already," I said. "Come, let's have a little treat."

So we take a walk, it's a nice day. We find a diner, nothing fancy, but clean and quiet. I try to buy her a piece of cake, a sandwich maybe, but no, all she wants is coffee.

So we sit and talk a little. She wants to know about my childhood in the old country, she wants to know about the boat ride to

America, she wants to know did my parents speak Yiddish to me when I was growing up. "Harry," she says to me, "when I hear old people talking Yiddish, it's like a love letter blowing in the wind. I try to run after them, and sometimes I catch a phrase that makes me cry or a word that makes me laugh. Even if I don't understand, it always touches my heart."

Oy, this teacher has some strange ideas. "Why do you want to speak Jewish?" I ask her. "Here in America, everybody speaks English. You don't need it. What's done is done, what's past is past. You shouldn't go with the old people so much. You should go out, make friends, have a good time. You got some troubles you want to talk about? Maybe I shouldn't pry," I say, "but you shouldn't look so sad, a young girl like you. When you're old you got plenty to be sad. You shouldn't think about the old days so much, let the dead rest in peace. What's done is done."

I took a swallow of my coffee, to calm down my nerves. I was getting a little too excited.

"Harry, listen to me," the teacher says. "I'm thirty years old and no one in my family will talk to me because I'm gay. It's all Harvey Milk's fault. He made such an impression on me. You know, when he died, what he said, 'If a bullet enters my brain, let that bullet destroy every closet door.' So when he died, I came out to everyone—the people at work, my parents. I felt it was my duty, so the Dan Whites of the world wouldn't be able to get away with it. I mean, if every single gay person came out— just think of it!— everyone would see they had a gay friend or a gay brother or a gay cousin or a gay teacher. Then they couldn't say things like 'Those gays should be shot.' Because they'd be saying you should shoot my neighbor or my sister or my daughter's best friend."

I never saw the teacher get so excited before. Maybe a politician she should be. She reminded me a little bit of Harvey.

"So *nu*, what's the problem?" I ask.

"The problem is my parents," she says with a sigh, and such a sigh I never heard from a young person before. "My parents haven't spoken to me since I told them I was gay. 'How could you do this to us?' they said. I wasn't doing anything to them. I tried to explain I couldn't help being gay, like I couldn't help being a Jew, but that they didn't want to hear. So I haven't spoken to them in eight years."

"Eight years, *Gottenyu*," I say to her. This I never heard in my whole life. A father and a mother cut off their own daughter like that. Better they should cut off their own hand. I thought about Gracie, a perfect daughter she's not, but your child is your child. When she married the *Goy*, Fannie threatened to put her head in the oven, but she got over it. Not to see your own daughter for eight years, and such a smart, gorgeous girl, such a good teacher, what a *shanda*.

So what can I do, I ask. Does she want me to talk to them, a letter maybe I could write. Does she want I should adopt her, the hell with them, I make a little joke. She smiles. "Just talking to you makes me feel better," she says. So *nu*, now I'm Harry the social worker. She says that's why she wants the old people's stories so much, she doesn't know nothing from her own family history. She wants to know about her own people, maybe write a book. But it's hard to get the people to talk to her, she says, she doesn't understand.

"Listen, Teacher," I tell her. "These old people have stories you shouldn't know from. What's there to tell? Hunger and more hunger. Suffering and more suffering. I buried my sister over twenty years ago, my mother, my father—all dead. You think I could just start talking about them like I just saw them yesterday? You think I don't think about them every day? Right here I keep them," I say, pointing to my heart. "I try to forget them, I should live in peace, the dead are gone. Talking about them won't bring them back. You want stories, go talk to somebody else. I ain't got no stories."

I sat down then. I didn't even know I was standing up, I got so excited. Everybody in the diner was looking at me, a crazy man shouting at a young girl.

Oy, and now the teacher was crying. "I'm sorry," I says to her. "You want another coffee?"

"No thanks, Harry," she says. "I'm sorry, too."

"Forget it. We can just pretend it never happened," I say, and then we go.

VI.

All this crazy writing has shaken me up inside a little bit. Yesterday I was walking home from the diner, I thought I saw Harvey walking in front of me. No, it can't be, I says to myself, and my heart started to pound so, I got afraid I shouldn't drop dead in the street from a heart attack. But then the man turned around and it wasn't Harvey. It didn't even look like him at all.

I got myself upstairs and took myself a pill, I could feel my pressure was going up. All this talk about the past—Fannie, Harvey, Frieda, my mother, my father—what good does it do? This teacher and her crazy ideas. Did I ever ask my mother, my father, what their childhood was like? What nonsense. Better I shouldn't know.

So today is Saturday, no writing class, but still I'm writing in this crazy notebook. I ask myself, Harry, what can I do to make you feel a little better? And I answer myself, make me a nice chicken soup.

You think an old man like me can't make chicken soup? Let me tell you, on all the holidays it was Harry that made the soup. Every *Pesach* it was Harry skimming the *shmaltz* from the top of the pot, it was Harry making the *kreplach*. I ask you, where is it written that a man shouldn't know from chicken soup?

So I take myself down to the store, I buy myself a nice chicken, some carrots, some celery, some parsley—onions I already got, parsnips I can do without. I'm afraid I shouldn't have a heart attack *shlepping* all that food up the steps, but thank God, I make it alright.

I put up the pot with water, throw everything in one-two-three, and soon the whole house smells from chicken soup.

I remember the time Harvey came to visit and there I was with my apron on, skimming the *shmaltz* from the soup. Did he kid me about that! The only way I could get him to keep still was to invite him to dinner. "Listen, Harvey," I says to him. "Whether you're a man or a woman, it doesn't matter. You gotta learn to cook. When you're old, nobody cares. Nobody will do for you. You gotta learn to do for yourself."

"I won't live past fifty, Har," he says, smearing a piece of rye bread with *shmaltz*.

"Nobody wants to grow old, believe me, I know," I says to him. "But listen, it's not so terrible. What's the alternative? Nobody wants to die young, either." I take off my apron and sit down with him.

"No, I mean it Harry," he says to me with his mouth full. "I won't make it to fifty. I've always known it. I'm a politician. A gay politician. Someone's gonna take a pot shot at me. It's a risk you gotta take."

The way he said it, I tell you, a chill ran down my back like I never felt before. He was forty-seven at the time, just a year before he died.

VII.

Today after the writing class, the teacher tells us she's going away for two days. Everyone makes a big fuss, the class they like so much already. She tells us she's sorry, something came up she has to do. She says we can come have class without her, the room will be open, we can read to each other what we write in our notebooks. Someone asks her what we should write about.

"Write me a letter," she says. "Write a story called 'What I Never Told Anyone'."

So, after everyone leaves, I ask her does she want to go out, have a coffee, but she says no, she has to go home and pack.

I tell her wherever she's going she should have a good time.

"Thanks, Harry," she says. "You'll be here when I get back?"

"Sure," I tell her. "I like this crazy writing. It passes the time."

She swings a big black bookbag onto her shoulder, a regular Hercules this teacher is, and she smiles at me. "I gotta run, Harry. Have a good week." She turns and walks away and something on her bookbag catches my eye. A big shiny pin that spells out her name all fancy-shmancy in rhinestones: Barbara. And under that, right away I see sewn onto her bookbag an upside-down pink triangle.

I stop in my tracks, stunned. No, it can't be, I says to myself. Maybe it's just a design? Maybe she doesn't know from this? My heart is beating fast now, I know I should go home, take myself a pill, my pressure, I can feel it going up.

But I just stand there. And then I get mad. What, she thinks maybe I'm blind as well as old, I can't see what's right in front of my nose? Or maybe we don't remember such things? What right does she have to walk in here with that, that thing on her bag, to remind us of what we been through? Haven't we seen enough?

Stories she wants. She wants we should cut our hearts open and give her stories so she could write a book. Well, alright, now I'll tell her a story.

This is what I never told anyone. One day, maybe seven, eight years ago—no, maybe longer, I think Harvey was still alive—one day Izzie comes knocking on my door. I open the door and there's Izzie, standing there, his face white as a sheet. I bring him inside, I make him a coffee. "Izzie, what is it," I says to him. "Something happened to the children, to the grandchildren, God forbid?"

He sits down, he doesn't drink his coffee. He looks through me like I'm not even there. Then he says, "Harry, I'm walking down the street, you know I had a little lunch at the Center, and then I come outside, I see a young man, maybe twenty-five, a good-looking guy, walking toward me. He's wearing black pants, a white shirt, and on his shirt he's got a pink triangle."

"So," I says. "A pink triangle, a purple triangle, they wear all kinds of crazy things these days."

"*Heshel*," he tells me, "don't you understand? The gays are wearing pink triangles just like the war, just like in the camps."

No, this I can't believe. Why would they do a thing like that? But if Izzie says it, it must be true. Who would make up such a thing?

"He looked a little bit like *Yussl*," Izzie says, and then he begins to cry, and such a cry like I never heard. Like a baby he was, with the tears streaming down his cheeks and his shoulders shaking with great big sobs. Such moans and groans I never heard from a grown man in all my life. I thought maybe he was gonna have a heart attack the way he was carrying on. I didn't know what to do. I was afraid the neighbors would hear, they shouldn't call the police, such sounds he was making. Fifty-eight years old he was, but he looked like a little boy sitting there, sniffling. And who was *Yussl*? Thirty years we'd been friends, and I never heard from *Yussl*.

So finally, I put my arms around him, and I held him, I didn't know what else to do. His body was shaking so, I thought his bones would crack from knocking against each other. Soon his body got quiet, but then all of a sudden his mouth got noisy.

"Listen, *Heshel*, I got to tell you something, something I never told nobody in my whole life. I was young in the camps, nineteen, maybe twenty when they took us away." The words poured from his mouth like a flood. "*Yussl* was my best friend in the camps. Already I saw my mother, my father, my Hannah marched off to the ovens. *Yussl* was the only one I had to hold on to.

"One morning, during the selection, they pointed me to the right, *Yussl* to the left. I went a little crazy, I ran after him. 'No, he stays with me, they made a mistake,' I said, and I grabbed him by the hand and dragged him back in line. Why the guard didn't kill us right then, I couldn't tell you. Nothing made sense in that place.

"*Yussl* and I slept together on a wooden bench. That night I couldn't sleep. It happened pretty often in that place. I would close my eyes and see such things that would make me scream in the night, and for that I could get shot. I don't know what was worse, asleep or awake. All I saw was suffering.

"On this night, *Yussl* was awake, too. He didn't move a muscle, but I could tell. Finally he said my name, just a whisper, but something broke in me and I began to cry. He put his arms around me and we cried together, such a close call we'd had.

"And then he began to kiss me. 'You saved my life,' he whispered, and he kissed my eyes, my cheeks, my lips. And Harry, I kissed him back. Harry, I never told nobody this before. I, we. . .we, you know, that was such a place that hell, I couldn't help it. The warmth of his body was just too much for me and Hannah was dead already and we would soon be dead too, probably, so what did it matter?"

He looked up at me then, the tears streaming from his eyes. "It's O.K., Izzie," I said. "Maybe I would have done the same."

"There's more, Harry," he says, and I got him a tissue, he should blow his nose. What more could there be?

"This went on for a couple of months maybe, just every once in a while when we couldn't sleep. He'd whisper my name and I'd answer with his, and then we'd, you know, we'd touch each other. We were very, very quiet, but who knows, maybe some other boys in the barracks were doing the same.

"To this day I don't know how it happened, but somehow someone found out. One day *Yussl* didn't come back to the barracks at night. I went almost crazy, you can imagine, all the things that went through my mind, the things they might have done to him, those lousy Nazis. I looked everywhere, I asked everyone, three days he was gone. And then on the third day, they lined us up after supper and there they had *Yussl*. I almost collapsed on the ground when I saw him. They had him on his knees with his hands tied behind his back. His face was swollen so, you couldn't even see his eyes. His clothes were stained with blood. And on his uniform they had sewn a pink triangle, big, twice the size of our yellow stars.

"*Oy*, did they beat him but good. 'Who's your friend?' they yelled at him. 'Tell us and we'll let you live.' But no, he wouldn't tell. He knew they were lying, he knew they'd kill us both. They asked him again and again, 'Who's your friend? Tell us which one he is.' And every time he said no, they'd crack him with a whip until the blood ran from him like a river. Such a sight he was, like I've never seen. How he remained conscious I'll never know.

"Everything inside me was broken after that. I wanted to run to his side, but I didn't dare, so afraid I was. At one point he looked at me, right in the eye, as though he was saying, *Izzie, save your-self. Me, I'm finished, but you, you got a chance to live through this and tell the world our story.*

"Right after he looked at me, he collapsed, and they shot him, Harry, right there in front of us. Even after he was dead they kicked him in the head a little bit. They left his body out there for two days, as a warning to us. They whipped us all that night, and from then on we had to sleep with all the lights on and with our hands on top of the blankets. Anyone caught with their hands under the blankets would be shot.

"He died for me, Harry, they killed him for that, was it such a terrible thing? *Oy*, I haven't thought about *Yussl* for twenty-five years maybe, but when I saw that kid on the street today, it was too much." And then he started crying again, and he clung to me like a child.

So what could I do? I was afraid he shouldn't have a heart attack, maybe he was having a nervous breakdown, maybe I should get the doctor. *Vay iss mir*, I never saw anybody so upset in my whole life. And such a story, *Gottenyu*.

"Izzie, come lie down," I says, and I took him by the hand to the bed. I laid him down, I took off his shoes, and still he was crying. So what could I do? I lay down with him, I held him tight. I told him he was safe, he was in America. I don't know what else I said, I don't think he heard me, still he kept crying.

I stroked his head, I held him tight. "Izzie, it's alright," I said. "Izzie, Izzie, *Izzaleh.*" I said his name over and over, like a lullaby, until his crying got quiet. He said my name once softly, *Heshel*, or maybe he said *Yussl*, I don't remember, but thank God he finally fell asleep. I tried to get up from the bed, but Izzie held onto me tight. So what could I do? Izzie was my friend for thirty years, for him I would do anything. So I held him all night long, and he slept like a baby.

And this is what I never told nobody, not even Harvey. That there in that bed, where Fannie and I slept together for forty-two years, me and Izzie spent the night. Me, I didn't sleep a wink, such a lump in my throat I had, like the night Harvey died.

Izzie passed on a couple months after that. I saw him a few more times, and he seemed different somehow. How, I couldn't say. We never talked about that night. But now that he had told someone his deepest secret, he was ready to go, he could die in peace. Maybe now that I told, I can die in peace, too?

VIII.

Dear Teacher:

You said write what you never told nobody, and write you a letter. I always did all my homework, such a student I was. So *nu*, I got to tell you something. I can't write in this notebook no more, I can't come no more to the class. I don't want you should take offense, you're a good teacher and a nice girl. But me, I'm an old man, I don't sleep so good at night, these stories are like a knife in my heart. Harvey, Fannie, Izzie, *Yussl*, my father, my mother, let them all rest in peace. The dead are gone. Better to live for today. What good does remembering do, it doesn't bring back the dead. Let them rest in peace.

But Teacher, I want you should have my notebook. It doesn't have nice stories in it, no love letters, no happy endings for a nice girl like you. A bestseller it ain't, I guarantee. Maybe you'll put it in a book someday, the world shouldn't forget.

Meanwhile, good luck to you, Teacher. May you live and be well and not get shot in the head like poor Harvey, may he rest in peace. Maybe someday we'll go out, have a coffee again, who knows? But me, I'm too old for this crazy writing. I remember too much, the pen is like a knife twisting in my heart.

One more thing, Teacher. Between parents and children, it's not so easy. Believe me, I know. Don't give up on them. One father, one mother, it's all you got. If you were my *tochter*, I'd be proud of you.

Harry

Only A Phase

I.

At 11:30 in the morning, Miriam Rosenfeld sat in the brown vinyl reclining chair she had bought her husband fifteen years ago for Father's Day, with her feet up and her head tilted slightly back. The TV was on, the curtains were drawn, and the burglar alarm was set. There was a cup of lukewarm instant coffee perched on a nearby end table, a lit Marlboro cigarette smoldering in an ashtray balanced on the arm of the chair, and a remote control for switching TV channels lying in her lap.

Miriam was knitting a tiny sweater. There was also a ball of yellow yarn in her lap, attached by a thin strand to the knitting needles she held in her two hands. The needles were constantly moving, and their incessant clicking was both comforting and annoying to the various members of Miriam's family, none of whom were home at 11:30 on a Tuesday morning except for Noodles, the family dog. Noodles lay in his customary spot, under the extended part of the recliner upon which Miriam rested her green fuzzy-slippered feet.

Every so often, Miriam pulled out more yarn from the ball on her lap by raising both her arms high over her head. Then she would lower her arms and wrap the loose strand of yarn around her left index finger which she kept stiff and pointing skyward as she continued to knit, barely missing a beat. Occasionally, Miriam interrupted herself to take a sip of coffee, puff on her cigarette, or change the TV channel by aiming the remote control at the set and pushing a button. Then she would squint at the screen across the room,

ignoring the glasses that dangled from a chain around her neck
and rested contentedly on her bosom. Miriam wore a green velour
bathrobe that matched her slippers. There were dark circles under her eyes.

At exactly noon, "The Price Is Right" was over and the news came
on. Miriam had no interest in the news—wars, killings, muggings
on the subways—you call that news? she'd ask her husband, who
always protested whenever Miriam pointed the remote control at
the set and zapped the evening news into "Laverne and Shirley."

In between the morning game shows and the afternoon soaps,
Miriam ignored the disasters of the world, and instead, let the dog
out, took in the mail, made herself a fresh cup of instant coffee,
and sometimes made a phone call or two. This week she had to
call the exterminator to take care of the ants in the kitchen, the
floor waxer to do the downstairs floors, the electrician to fix the light
over the garage, and the mechanic to see if he had time to give her
car a tune-up. Sighing, Miriam put down her knitting and started
to get up from her chair. Then, changing her mind, she settled back
down again and held her work up to the light for inspection.

"Not bad, if I do say so myself," Miriam said to no one in particular, pulling at a small yellow sleeve. She was making a sweater for
Esther's grandchild, her third, due in two weeks. Miriam wondered
whether it would be a boy or a girl, and hoped for a boy, for Esther's sake. Boys were so much easier. She *futzed* with the sweater
a minute longer, then put it down, and with an *oy!*, heaved herself
out of the reclining chair, which snapped into an upright position.
Noodles bounded out from under the chair, his tail high in the air,
his head tilted slightly to one side. A walk maybe? Or better yet,
some lunch? Perhaps both. This was the extent of the possibilities
that existed in his little canine mind.

"Oh Noodles, I'm ti-re-d." Miriam let out a big yawn, stretching
her words instead of her body. "Come here, Noodles. Where's that
Noodle-Poodle? Let Mama see her good boy. Such a good boy." She
bent down and stroked Noodles' curly grey head. Noodles, lulled
by Miriam's voice, lay himself down and rolled over, presenting his
belly to her as a token of undying, everlasting love. Miriam petted
the dog for a minute, and then with another *oy!* straightened up.
Noodles leapt to his feet as well.

"Good boy," Miriam repeated. "Wanna go out?" At those words, Noodles made a dash for the front door and stood there waiting, his little pompom of a tail wagging furiously and an occasional impatient yelp escaping from his mouth.

"I'm coming, Noodles. Mama's coming. Hold your horses." Ignoring the advice she used to give to the children—pick up your feet. Walk like a *mensh!*—Miriam shuffled down the hallway to the front door.

"O.K., O.K., does Noodles want to go out?" Miriam turned to a panel on the wall, where a small red light glowed eerily through the semi-dark hallway. She turned a key that changed the light from red to green, signaling that the burglar alarm was disengaged. Then she opened the front door and stood in the door frame, one foot inside the house and the other on the cement path. Noodles ran past her, and commenced his morning ritual of cautiously sniffing the shrubbery and raising his rear left leg every few feet.

Miriam shifted her weight so that she could reach into the mailbox for the mail. Cradling it in her arms, she narrowed her eyes at the day, waiting for Noodles to finish his business. It was mid-April, and there was still a chill in the morning air, though here and there a bird sang sweetly, and a few crocuses had already popped their little purple heads up through the neighbor's front yard.

After a minute, Miriam called out, "*Nu*, Noodles? C'mon boy. In the house. Let's go." The dog appeared in a second, his tail high and his walk bouncier than it had been a few minutes before.

"Did you make? What a good boy. You're such a good boy." Miriam held open the door as Noodles trotted past. Turning her back on the day, Miriam entered the house, shut the door firmly behind her, and turned the key in the wall, resetting the burglar alarm. Then she walked into the kitchen, where Noodles was waiting expectantly.

"Do you want your crackers, you good boy? Is that what you want?" Dropping the mail onto the kitchen table, Miriam reached up into a cabinet for a red box. She pulled out three crackers shaped like firemen and tossed them to Noodles who promptly devoured them, and then, tail high and nose low, proceeded to conduct a thorough investigation of the kitchen, searching for stray People

Cracker crumbs, signs of last night's dinner, or remnants of the sesame seed bagel Miriam's husband had had for breakfast that morning.

Left to her own devices, Miriam took a cup down from the cabinet, dumped a spoonful of coffee and emptied a packet of Sweet 'n' Low into it, and turned the flame on under the tea kettle. She put a cigarette into her mouth and bent over the stove to light it from the burner. Then she sat down to sift through the mail.

There was the *TV Guide*, a flyer from JC Penney's announcing their annual spring sale, the synagogue's monthly newsletter, an invitation to Irma and Stanley's thirty-fifth wedding anniversary, a bill from the oil company, and a letter from Deborah.

Miriam exhaled a long stream of smoke from her nostrils and stared at the envelope in her hand addressed to Ms. Miriam Rosenfeld and Mr. Seymour Rosenfeld. Would it kill Deborah to stick in that little *r* between the capital *M* and small *s*, and address her mother by the title she so rightfully deserved? No, Deborah had to do everything her way; she was as stubborn as the day was long.

Miriam took another puff from her cigarette and stared at the handwriting on the envelope for a moment, as if it held some clue to the contents inside. It was the first letter Deborah had written them in a long time, in almost a year. Maybe she was writing to tell them she had met a nice Jewish doctor and was bringing him home for *Pesach*. Maybe they were even engaged. Miriam doubted it, but you never know. She hoped Deborah wasn't sick, or God forbid, pregnant. She opened the envelope, unfolded the letter, and held it away from her at arm's length, as though it were something distasteful to the touch. She squinted at Deborah's curly handwriting which was not unlike her own, trying to make out the words. After a minute she gave in, unfolded her glasses, slid them up her nose and began to read:

> Dear Mom, Dad, and Noodles,
>
> Hi! I hope you are all well and happy. I know I haven't written for a while and I'm sorry about that. I know it must have hurt you, but that's not what I intended. I just needed some time to figure some things out.
>
> I haven't been exactly honest with you lately. I haven't lied exactly, but I haven't told the whole truth either. You know

when you call and ask me how's everything and what's new, and I say everything's fine and nothing's new? Well, that's not exactly so.

Everything is fine. As a matter of fact, I'm happier than I've ever been. And a lot is new. I went through a rough period for a little while, but I am doing what I think is right, and what I believe in, just like you always taught me to.

What I am trying to tell you is this: I am a lesbian. I've known it for a while and now I want you to know it too. I'm tired of hiding the things that are important to me from you. I'm tired of the silence and distance that has grown between us. I hope that my taking this risk will bring us closer. I want you to know who I am. I trust that your love for me is real, and that you will accept me as I am, even if that is different than how you want me to be.

I'm happier than I ever imagined I could be, ever since I came out, and I know that is what you want for me (to be happy I mean). I still love you, that hasn't changed. Please write or call me so we can discuss this, or anything else.

Love to Grandma and Grandpa.

Love,
Deborah

The tea kettle was whistling shrilly, sending a blast of steam up through its spout into the still kitchen air. In fact, the water had been boiling for the last five minutes, but Miriam didn't seem to hear it. Finally she got up and turned off the stove, but she didn't pour the hot water into the open mouth of the waiting cup.

Instead she sat back down at the kitchen table, her feet flat on the floor, forming a perfect pillow upon which Noodles immediately lay his head. Miriam slipped her glasses off her nose, and let them hang idly around her neck. She stared at Deborah's letter again, not seeing the words this time, but seeing Deborah's face—not her twenty-six-year-old face, but her two-year-old face with her auburn hair in tiny wisps around her head, her green eyes fringed with long dark lashes, and that toothless grin that even strangers in the street would stop to admire.

"My baby," Miriam whispered, reaching out her hand as if she could somehow enfold Deborah into her arms. My only daughter, my baby girl. Miriam remembered the day Deborah was born, and how she had cried with joy to have finally produced a girl—a little miniature of herself, with ten perfect fingers and ten perfect toes, and those huge green eyes, though God knows where she had gotten them from—certainly not her side of the family. Miriam was crying now as well, big fat tears streaming from her eyes. She wiped her face with the back of her hand and stared at the letter again, seeing Deborah's face once more.

This time though, Deborah's tiny infant face dissolved and then reappeared as adult Deborah, looking somewhat hostile and somewhat vulnerable, as she had when she came home to visit two *Pesachs* ago. She had cut off almost all her beautiful auburn hair, and she wore a red T-shirt under black overalls with no brassière underneath. Miriam had been so excited that Deborah was coming home for the holidays that she had resolved not to nag her about anything, and she was all ready to greet her with a big hug and kiss. But when she opened the door and saw her daughter looking like something the cat had just dragged in, she had been forced to greet her coldly and bring her upstairs to change her clothes before, God forbid, any of the relatives got a chance to see her looking like that. Miriam had made Deborah borrow one of her own dresses to wear to dinner, but with her black sneakers she had still looked ridiculous. Why couldn't she be more like Esther's daughter, Miriam often lamented. Esther's daughter Irene had married a nice Jewish boy, an engineer, and had already given her two grandchildren, both boys.

But not Deborah. She had been trouble from the first—always wanting to do things her way or not at all, insisting on going to that *meshugeneh* college way up in Maine in the middle of nowhere, where they didn't even give out grades for all the money they charged, then living in that filthy hippie commune, and now. . . now this.

She has absolutely no sense, Miriam thought, suddenly feeling angry. Never did and never will. Always trying the newest thing; putting three holes in each ear lobe, smoking marijuana, and now this. Why, if the latest thing was wearing a frying pan on your head and walking up Fifth Avenue stark naked, that kid would probably do it.

Miriam folded the letter carefully, returned it to its envelope, and put it in her bathrobe pocket. I'll be damned if I'm going to show this to Seymour, she thought, stacking the rest of the mail into a neat pile. As if he doesn't have enough on his mind. It would kill him. She was always his favorite, Daddy's little girl. How dare she write us such a letter? Hasn't she put us through enough? What a rotten kid. She never thinks of anyone but herself.

Miriam sat at the kitchen table with Noodles dozing at her feet, for a long time, not making her phone calls, not drinking coffee, not knitting, not smoking cigarettes. She just stared at the yellow oilcloth covering the table. Once the phone rang and Noodles picked up his head, but Miriam didn't answer it.

At 3:00 the familiar voice of Mike Douglas, blaring from the TV set in the next room, seeped into Miriam's consciousness. Seymour would be home in two hours. She had to get dressed, straighten up the house a little, make supper. I'm not going to let that lousy kid ruin my life, she thought, placing both hands on the table and pushing herself up into a standing position. It's only a phase. She'll get over it, she told herself, as she took two sirloin patties out of the refrigerator. Then she shuffled down the hallway toward the bedroom to get dressed, the dog, as always, right at her heels.

II.

At exactly 4:31, Deborah Rosenfeld looked back over her right shoulder, pulled her car out of its parking space, and headed for home. She drove with the windows wide open and the tape deck blaring out Alive's newest album so loudly that when she stopped at a red light, the people in the car next to her turned their heads to stare. Ignoring them, Deborah kept her eyes fixed on the traffic light, her right hand on the stickshift, so she could switch gears and peel out as soon as the light changed, singing along with Rhiannon at the top of her lungs.

As she drove along, Deborah felt along the passenger seat for a pack of Chiclets. She chewed gum constantly, a habit that was both annoying and endearing to her various friends and coworkers. In addition to the box of Chiclets, a pair of mirror sunglasses, a pen, three quarters, two dimes, and a parking ticket lay on the front seat. Without taking her eyes off the road, Deborah's right hand located the box of gum, opened the flap, removed two pieces, shifted the car into fourth gear, and popped the gum into her mouth. Then she shifted her weight forward and pushed the box of gum down into her hip pocket. Deborah was wearing tight black chino pants, a white button-down shirt, a jeans jacket, and a pair of red Reebok sneakers. She also had five earrings on: two silver studs, two small hoops, and a silver snake that slithered from her left ear lobe almost down to her shoulder.

The music ended when she was almost home, and the tape deck automatically spit out the tape and switched the radio on. Deborah groaned and turned it off. She hated listening to the news—war, killings, rapes—the same thing every day. It's too depressing, she always said to her girlfriend, who liked to listen to the six o'clock report over dinner.

Deborah drove the rest of the way in silence, compiling a mental list of all the phone calls she had to make when she got home. She had to call Fotomat to see if her pictures were back yet, call Wendy about the Gay Pride posters, call the phone company about last month's screwed-up bill, and call Anita to see if she could reschedule her acupuncture appointment.

She swung into the driveway, turned off the car, and pulled up the emergency brake. Then Deborah gathered up her shoulderbag and a magazine from the back seat, opened the car door, and thrust first one leg, and then the other, out of the car. Standing up, she inspected the day. The sun was low in the sky, but the day still had some warmth left to it. One of the neighborhood kids rode by on a bicycle, his jacket balled up in the handlebar basket—a sure sign of spring. Deborah wished she didn't have to miss the best part of the day by being stuck in an office from 8:30 to 4:30, but at least for now, that's the way it was.

As she walked toward the back steps that led to her apartment, a grey and white cat ran up to greet her.

"Sushi! Hi there, Sushi. How's my Sushi-Pushi?" Sushi rubbed herself against Deborah's ankles, and Deborah bent down to scratch her between the ears.

"How's my girl, huh? How's my Sushi? Are you my best girl? Are you hungry? Come, I'll give you some supper. Let's go. In the house." Deborah rubbed Sushi at the base of her spine, causing her tail to stick straight up in the air. "*Oy*, I'm tired," she said, straightening up. Then she headed up the steps, with Sushi following behind.

Deborah stood on the back porch for a moment, fumbling with her keys. Sushi, not being big on patience, calmly pushed open the hinged cat-door Deborah had fastened for her, and went inside. A minute later, Deborah entered to find Sushi sitting right next to her supper bowl, her big green eyes staring at Deborah's hands, which she knew would eventually hold a can opener and a can of Nine Lives. Would it be Chicken and Cheese tonight? Or Tuna and Egg? Perhaps both. Sushi narrowed her eyes to concentrate on all the possibilities that existed in her little feline mind.

Deborah threw her keys and magazine on the kitchen table, and slung her shoulderbag on the back of a chair. "Did you make today, Sushi? Let's see." She went into the bathroom to inspect the litter box. "What a good cat. Clean as a whistle. Did you go outside? Good girl," Deborah crooned, bending down to scratch Sushi behind the ears again. Then she walked down the hallway into her bedroom to see if anyone had left a message on her answering machine.

The red light, glowing eerily through the semi-dark room, blinked three times, then paused, then blinked three times again, signaling three calls had been recorded. Deborah sat down on the edge of her bed, rewound the tape, and turned the knob to Playback Messages. Then she sat back with a pen and notebook in her hand. Sushi, realizing that dinner was temporarily postponed, sauntered into the bedroom, jumped up on Deborah's lap, and began to purr.

"Beep. Hello, this is Joan from Fotomat calling. Your pictures are ready. Thank you."

"Beep. Hi, Deb, this is Marcia. Wanna go see *Desert Hearts* tomorrow night? We can go to the late show. I'll even cook dinner for you. Call me. Bye."

"Beep. Deborah, you're never home. I'm sick of this machine. *Kvetch, kvetch, kvetch.* Listen, I'll be over at 6:30 with a surprise for you. What's for dinner? Can't wait. Bye. Oh, in case you're wondering, this is your girlfriend."

"Beep." A long dial tone followed, and then silence. Deborah turned the know to Answer Calls, and the little light on the machine turned green. Then she shifted her weight and gently nudged Sushi off her lap. Sushi, annoyed by this gesture and by the fact that her dinner had yet to appear, turned her back on Deborah in a huff and started lazily licking her right front paw.

"Oh Sushi, don't give me the cold shoulder. C'mon, let's see if we got any mail." Deborah opened the front door and walked down the steps that led to the lobby of her apartment building, Sushi trotting after her. She opened the box, took out the mail, then reached all the way inside, making sure she didn't miss anything. Satisfied, Deborah climbed the steps and waited for Sushi who was busy sniffing around a dusty corner of the hall. Deborah stood in the hallway, cradling the mail in her arms. "C'mon Sushi. C'mon. Here Sushi-shi-shi-shi-shi. You're a good cat. Let's go now." Sushi bounded up the stairs and walked through the door Deborah was holding open, her tail swishing behind her.

"Do you want your supper, you good cat? Is that what you want?" Deborah followed the cat into the kitchen, dumped the mail onto the table, and finally took off her jacket. She reached up into a cabinet for a can of Nine Lives, opened it, and plopped two spoonfuls into Sushi's dish. Sushi crouched in front of the bowl and began eating noisily, her metal pet tag clinking against her glass bowl.

The cat taken care of, Deborah took a mug down from the shelf, threw an Almond Sunset tea bag into it, and poured in a spoonful of honey. Then she turned the flame on under the tea kettle, popped a fresh piece of gum into her mouth, and sat down at the kitchen table to sort through the mail.

There was the latest issue of *off our backs*, a flyer from the women's bookstore announcing their annual spring sale, the Lesbian Alliance's monthly newsletter, an invitation to Melanie's thirty-fifth birthday party, a bill from the gas company, and a letter from her mother. Deborah cracked her gum extra loudly as she stared at the envelope in her hand, addressed to Miss Deborah Rosenfeld. Would it kill her mother to write *Ms.* like the rest of the human race? It's the 1980s for God's sake, Deborah thought. Even the office where she worked used *Mr.* or *Ms.* on all their forms. But no, not her mother. She had to do everything her way. She was as stubborn as a mule.

Deborah stared at the handwriting on the envelope, as if it held some clue to the contents inside. She had never expected her mother to write back so soon; she had sent her parents the letter only a week ago. Maybe her mother was writing to say, "*Mazel tov!* You're gay! Why didn't you tell us before?" Maybe she would even offer to throw her a coming out party. Deborah doubted it, but you never know. She hoped her mother wasn't going to disown her, or God forbid, sit *shiva* for a week. She opened the envelope, unfolded the letter, and held it up close to her face, trying to make out the words written in a curly handwriting that was not unlike her own. After a minute she gave up, reached into her shoulderbag, and pulled out her glasses from a black case that had a lavender women's symbol embroidered on it. She slipped the glasses onto her face, picked up the letter, and began to read:

Dear Deborah,

Thank you for being so honest with us. As you have set such a fine example, I will be honest as well and tell you that you are the most self-centered, self-absorbed, selfish person that I have ever met. I don't understand how two such decent people like your father and I could have raised such a daughter. Don't you ever think about anyone but yourself? How could you do this to us? You do not live in a vacuum you know. If you would only stop and think for a minute, which I suppose is too much to ask, you would see that your actions have serious consequences.

I will not call you to "discuss this or anything else." Thank you very much for the invitation. I have not shown your letter to your father, nor do I intend to do so. The least you could have done was think about him. He has enough things on his mind right now.

Grandma and Grandpa are fine. I trust you will have the decency not to say anything about this to them. Deborah, where is your head? You never did have any sense.

Noodles is fine and sends love.

Be well,
your mother

The tea kettle was whistling shrilly, sending a blast of steam up through its spout into the still kitchen air. In fact, the water had been boiling for the last five minutes, though Deborah didn't seem to hear it. Finally she got up and turned off the stove, but she didn't pour the hot water into the open mouth of the waiting mug. Instead she sat back down at the kitchen table, her thighs pressed together, making a perfect bed for Sushi to hop up onto and lay down on. Deborah took her glasses off and put them upside down on the table. She stared at her mother's letter again, not seeing the words this time, but seeing her mother's face. Not her fifty-year-old face, but the young face that had hovered over two-year-old Deborah, like the brightest star at night, singing a special lullaby just for her.

"My mommy," Deborah whispered, reaching out her hand as if she could somehow find her mother's skirts and cling to them. Deborah remembered all the times her mother had kissed away her tears; when she fell in the park and cut her knee on some broken glass, when the boys at school teased her for being a carrot-top, and the time the science project she had worked so hard on only placed third in the school's science fair. Deborah was crying now as well, big fat tears streaming from her eyes. She wiped her tears with the back of her hand and stared at the letter again seeing her mother's face once more.

This time, though, Deborah saw her mother as she had looked two years ago, the last time she had seen her, when she went home to visit for *Pesach*. Deborah had resolved to be pleasant to her mother and not criticize her about anything. She had even bought a black velour sleeveless jumpsuit and a red shirt to wear, which Roberta assured her looked just fine. But when her mother had met her at the door with that look of absolute disgust on her face and then actually made her put on a dress that was way too big for her and looked ridiculous with her unshaved legs and high-top sneakers, Deborah had had no choice but to remain cool and aloof for the entire visit. Why couldn't her mother be more like Melanie's mother? Roxanne didn't care that her daughter was a lesbian. In fact, she had marched in Gay Pride last year carrying a sign that said, *Hip Hip Hooray, My Daughter's Gay!* She'd probably even be at Melanie's birthday party.

My mother's always been impossible, Deborah thought. Always trying to make me do things her way—go to an ivy league school, marry a nice Jewish boy, have a bunch of kids. She was completely close-minded, Deborah thought, feeling angry. Why, if chastity belts were still around, my mother would probably make me wear one. And if she really had her way, she probably would have gone to a *shadchen* and arranged a match for me a long time ago.

Deborah folded the letter carefully, returned it to its envelope, and put it in her back pocket. How dare she write me such a letter, she thought, glancing for a minute at the rest of the mail. She's called me names my whole life. She's the one who's selfish, always thinking about herself—herself and what the neighbors will say.

Deborah sat at the kitchen table with Sushi snoozing on her lap, not drinking tea, chewing gum, or making phone calls. She just stared at the texture of the two straw place mats on the kitchen table. Once the phone rang and Sushi's ears twitched in her sleep, but Deborah let the answering machine get it.

At 5:45 Deborah looked up at the clock. Roberta would be over in forty-five minutes. She had to get out of these work clothes, straighten up the house a little, and make supper. I'm not going to let my mother ruin my Friday night, she thought, as she lifted Sushi off her lap, placed both hands on the kitchen table, and pushed herself up into a standing position. It's only a phase. She'll get over it, she told herself, as she put up a pot of water for the spaghetti. Then she walked down the hallway toward her bedroom to change her clothes, the cat, as always, trailing right behind.

One *Shabbos* Evening

for A., with much love

Lydia had just finished setting the table with her only two match-ing plates and bowls when the doorbell rang. She glanced at the clock and smiled to herself as she hurried to open the door. Exact-ly 5:55. Emily was the only other dyke she knew who was compul-sively early, just like herself. That's why they were best friends.

"Hi, *mameleh*," Lydia said, as she pulled open the door.

"Hi, *bubbeleh*," Emily answered, handing Lydia a white paper bag that was sitting on her lap. "Here, take these," she said, as Lydia stepped aside and Emily wheeled past her into the apartment.

Lydia followed Emily down the hallway back to the kitchen, open-ing the top of the paper bag and sticking her nose inside. "Quelle *shayna* bagels," she said, pulling out a fat whole-wheat and raisin bagel and placing it in the basket on the table. She pulled out two more, and frowned at Emily who was wiggling out of her coat.

"Emily, did you get all whole-wheat and raisin?"

Emily twisted around in her wheelchair to get a small brown bag out of the blue pouch that was hanging behind her from two small straps looped over the handles of her chair. "I didn't want you to have a fit, so I went to Waldbaums and got you an onion bagel and some cream cheese." She opened the bag and put its contents on the table along with a stick of soy margarine. "I don't know why you insist on having white flour and dairy every Friday night when you know how bad it is for you."

"*Oy*, Emily, such a *goyishe kop* you have." Lydia bent down and kissed the top of Emily's head. "A whole-wheat and raisin bagel is like whole-wheat and raisin spaghetti. *Feh*." She took Emily's coat from her and went to hang it in the hall closet. "Once a week

I live a little," she called over her shoulder. "It didn't do my grandfather any harm, and he lived to be eighty-seven."

"I can't hear you," Emily called, as she wheeled over to the stove and lifted the lid off a big soup pot. A cloud of steam immediately enveloped her. "Umm. The soup smells great," Emily said, as Lydia came back into the room. "Let's light the candles and eat."

Lydia put two white candles into a pair of brass candlesticks and placed them on the table. She lit one, Emily lit the other, and both women made three wide circles in the air with their hands, bathing themselves in the *Shabbos* light. They sang the blessing and kissed each other on both cheeks, saying *Shabbot sholom*. Then Emily wheeled to her place at the table, and Lydia filled their bowls with chicken soup and sat down.

"So what's new?" Emily asked, dividing a *matzo* ball in half with the edge of her spoon.

"Well, Em, I've got a completely fabulous idea." Lydia reached across Emily's bowl for a bottle of seltzer. "You know that *klezmer* band we saw a few weeks ago, the one with that great singer, the blonde, what's-her-name?"

"Judy, I think it is."

"Yeah, Judy." Lydia filled her glass with seltzer. "Well, I've been thinking that we should have a lesbian *klezmer* band. Wouldn't that be great? And I've got the perfect name for it, too." Lydia's eyes twinkled in the light of the *Shabbos* candles as she looked up at Emily. "Are you ready?"

"No, let me guess." Emily reached for a whole wheat bagel, put it on her plate, and began slicing it in half. "The *Yentes*?"

"No." Lydia shook her head vigorously. "You'll never guess."

Emily put down her knife and fingered the maroon scarf she was wearing around her neck. "The Dyke Kikes?" she asked.

"Emily, that's gross." Lydia shook her head again, slowly this time. "It's a good thing you're Jewish, otherwise I'd give you such a *zetz*. . . ."

Emily laughed. "You sound just like my mother."

"*Essen in gezunt, meyn klayne kind*." Lydia put another bagel on Emily's plate, which Emily promptly removed. "So, do you give up?" she asked hopefully.

"I guess so."

Lydia put down the chicken wing she was gnawing on and executed a drum roll on the table with the tips of her fingers. "Ladies and jellybeans, may I present . . . the fabulous . . . Klezbians!"

"The Klezbians?" Emily repeated.

"Yeah, Emily, don't you get it? *Klezmer* plus lesbian equals . . ."

"Yeah, I get it, I get it. But who's going to be in it?"

"Well, let's see." Lydia stared for a moment at her curved reflection on the back of her silver soup spoon. Her face flattened out behind a huge nose and she flared her nostrils at herself a few times before turning her spoon around and dipping it back into her soup. "We'll need a horn player, a few fiddles, a drummer maybe, a flute. . . ."

"How about a triangle? I used to play the triangle in second grade."

"Great, Emily. I was counting on you to be in it." Lydia put her spoon down, picked up her bowl with both hands, and raised it to her lips, noisily slurping down the rest of her soup.

"Aren't you forgetting something?" Emily asked, as Lydia's face reappeared from behind her bowl.

"What?"

"Who's going to sing? Not that Judy girl, unless you know something I don't."

"I wish." Lydia sighed and unbuttoned the top two buttons of her purple velour pullover. The chicken soup was making her hot. "Did you ever see such a pair of gorgeous arms in your whole life? *Oy*, when she walked out on stage in that sleeveless blue sequin top, I almost *plotzed*." A faraway look came into Lydia's eyes for a moment. Then she sighed again, bringing herself to the present. "Oh well. I never did like blondes much anyway." Lydia took her onion bagel from the basket, cut it in half and spread some cream cheese on it. "Maybe she'll teach me how to sing, though."

"You're going to sing?" Emily rolled her eyes.

"Yeah. What are you making such a *punim* for?" Lydia gestured at Emily with the knife in her hand.

"Lydia, in the first place, much as I love you, you can't carry a tune. And in the second place, you don't know Yiddish."

"So." Lydia's lower lip began to pout. "I can learn, you know. Besides, I do so know a *bisseleh* Yiddish." She jumped up from her seat and pointed at the table. "*Dos iz meyn tish, und dos iz meyn tush.*" She put her hands on her hips, turned around and wiggled her behind. Emily laughed. Then Lydia crossed the room and took something out of the freezer. "*Dos iz meyn fish,*" she said, holding up a piece of frozen haddock, "*und dos iz meyn fus.*" She lifted her left foot and pointed. Then she put the haddock back in the freezer and sat down again, smiling broadly at Emily. "See?"

"I'm impressed. You're practically fluent," Emily said, tilting her bowl toward her and pouring the last drop of soup into her spoon.

"I've even written a song already," Lydia informed her proudly.

"In Yiddish?" Emily's eyebrows rose.

"Partly."

"*Oy.* This I've got to hear. Are you going to sing it to me?"

"Maybe. If you're a good girl and finish the rest of your bagel."

"*Oy,* Lydia, you're sounding more and more like a Jewish mother everyday, you should pardon the expression."

"Well, I have to practice. I will be one someday, if I find the comother of my dreams." Lydia stood up and reached for Emily's bowl. "Want more soup?"

"No thanks. Well, yeah, give me another *knaydlach.*"

"*Knaydl,* Emily. *Knaydlach* is plural." Lydia went over to the stove and ladled some soup into Emily's bowl. Emily stared at her back. "You have been studying Yiddish," she said, with a note of surprise.

"Yeah, I'm serious," she said, setting Emily's bowl down in front of her. "I want to learn to speak the language of our grandmothers, Em. You know, language says so much about a culture. Like . . . ," she paused for a minute, "like, 'Will you sit over there?' sounds a lot different from '*zich zetzen dortn.*' "

"Where'd you learn that?" Emily asked.

"*Ich hob a buch.*" Lydia turned from the stove where she was filling her own bowl, and set her soup down on the table. Then she leaned over and picked up a book from the windowsill. "I have a book," she repeated, handing it to Emily and sitting down.

"*The Yiddish Teacher,*" Emily read aloud. She flipped through the book for a minute, staring at the Hebrew letters which were meaningless to her. She pushed the book over toward Lydia. "What gives with the Yiddish?" she asked.

Lydia stroked the cover of the book gently, as though it was a be-loved cat. "I don't know, Em. That concert really moved me. You know, just hearing the sound of the words was like coming home. It must be in my genes or something." She stopped stroking the book and looked up at Emily. "And no, I don't mean in my pants."

"You read my mind." Emily grinned.

"I know. So anyway," Lydia continued, "I bought a *klezmer* tape, and I've been listening to it in my car every day on my way to work. It's like a private twenty-minute total immersion class. And then I got this book, and I've taught myself the alphabet and now I can even pick out a few words in the songs," Lydia said proudly.

"*Mazel tov.*" Emily picked up a black and white salt shaker shaped like a penguin and shook it over her soup. "I still don't see what the point of all this is."

"The point is. . . ." Lydia paused again, knowing that words couldn't explain this passion that had suddenly emerged in her. "The point is, Emily, that English is a foreign language to me. To you, too, you know. I want to speak to my grandmother in her own language, in our own language, just once before she dies."

Lydia looked at Emily intently. "I don't know. Maybe I'm a little *meshugeh*. But I have this mad yearning to learn Yiddish. You know, I'm really good at languages, like that summer I lived in Mexico, I picked up Spanish really fast. The trouble is, there's no place left to go to be totally immersed in Yiddish anymore."

Emily took a bite of her bagel and chewed thoughtfully. "How about Miami Beach?" she asked.

"Oh Emily, I'm serious."

"So am I."

"Well, I'm not going to Miami Beach. I'm going to work with my book and then take a course at the university and probably go to New York next summer. Columbia has a six-week Yiddish program that's supposed to be terrific."

Emily wrinkled up her nose. "New York in the summer? Lydia, are you out of your mind? You wouldn't last a week."

"Emily, why are you being so unsupportive?" Lydia looked direct-ly in Emily's eyes, which were a dark liquid brown that always reminded her of milk chocolate.

"I don't know. I just don't understand why you want to learn Yiddish. You speak with your grandmother perfectly well in English. Yiddish is a dead language." She stared back into Lydia's eyes which were also brown, though lighter than her own, and flecked with bits of gold.

"Emily, that's a rotten thing to say." Lydia reached across the table for the penguin saltshaker, and rolled it back and forth between her hands. "You know, when I lived in Mexico I met this Spanish woman, and we talked a little in English. It was when I first got there. Then she turned away to talk to some of her friends and then she turned back to me. 'I'm sorry,' she said, 'I understand English, but when I speak in my own language, I understand in brighter colors.' I never forgot that, Emily. I want to understand the brighter colors of my grandmother's life."

"I'm sorry." Emily took the penguin peppershaker off the table and stared at it. It was wearing a red bowtie. "I'm just worried where all this Jewish stuff is taking you, Lydia. I'm scared I'll show up here one Friday night and you'll answer the door with a shaved head and a *sheytl* and seventeen kids and a husband off in *shul* and then you'll move to Israel and then . . ."

"Emily are you serious?" Lydia set the saltshaker down on the table with a thump. "Em, going straight is the farthest thing from my mind, believe me. That's not what this is all about." She shook her head in disbelief. "Can you imagine me with a guy, Emily? Me? The woman who'd be happy if she never saw a man naked from the neck down again?" Lydia leaned forward in her chair. "Emily, I've been listening to that tape in my car every morning now for three weeks, and every single day it makes me cry. Really. I've had to tell them at work I've suddenly developed these strange allergies, so they don't think I'm losing my mind. I come in and my eyes are always full of tears." Lydia put her hand on Emily's arm. "It pulls at my heartstrings, Emily, and I just have to go with it."

"Well, don't go too far," Emily said, covering Lydia's hand with her own. "Judaism is just so entrenched with heterosexism. I can't even get near it for two seconds before I start feeling guilty for not perpetuating the race."

"I know what you mean." Lydia nodded her head. "But there are some gay synagogues. And I'm going to have a Jewish baby, even

if it is with a turkey baster. You just have to find your own balance."
Lydia paused for a minute as she stood up and started clearing the
table. "Like having *Shabbos* dinner with me every Friday night,
Em. That's perpetuating the culture at least." She carried the dishes
over to the sink. "Anyway, you shaved your head at Michigan last
summer."

"But that was different." Emily ran her fingers through her thick
black hair, which was still quite short.

"Don't worry, Emily. I'm not going to desert you for the wonderful world of heterosexuality." Lydia returned to the table and began wiping it with a sponge.

"I certainly hope not," Emily said, leaning down and pulling back
the two levers that released her rear wheels. She backed up her chair
and then moved forward, picking up the cream cheese and soy margarine and putting them into the refrigerator.

"I'll sing you my song, then you'll feel better," Lydia said, letting
the water run in the sink. "Want some coffee or tea?" she asked
Emily.

"No, let's go sit in the living room." Emily wheeled through the
kitchen doorway and Lydia followed.

"I'll be right in," Lydia called, as she ducked into her bedroom
for a minute. Then, carrying a blue spiral notebook, she entered
the living room, to find Emily picking dead leaves off her philoden-
dron plant.

"Lyd, you have to stop watering this plant so much. You're drown-
ing the poor thing." Emily turned her chair and crossed the room,
her lap full of withered yellow leaves. "Look at this."

"Oh, I thought I wasn't watering it enough and that's why it was
dying." Lydia dropped her notebook onto the couch, bent over in
front of the stereo, and started thumbing through some records,
while Emily returned to the kitchen to get rid of the dead leaves.
"I'm just going to play you a song or two, to get you in the mood,"
she said, as Emily came back.

Emily clasped her hands in front of her heart, and began to sing,
in her best Perry Como imitation: "I'm in the mood for Jews. Simply because you're near me. Honey, but when you're near me, I'm
in the mood for Jews."

"At least one of us can carry a tune," Lydia said as she turned the stereo on.

"Well, you can tune a fork but you can't tuna fish, har har har," Emily said, popping a wheely in the middle of the floor.

"Emily, don't do that. You know it gives me a heart attack." Lydia covered her eyes as Emily thrust herself forward and then leaned back, balancing herself up on her two rear wheels for a minute before coming back down.

"Can't a girl have any fun around here?" she asked, spinning around in a circle. "Alright, alright, I'll behave." She brought herself to a stop, right in front of Lydia. "What have you got there?"

"It's the *klezmer* band's second album. I got it at the library." Lydia handed her the cover and lowered the needle in the groove between the third and fourth songs. "This is called '*Mazel Tov Dances*,' " she said, stepping back. Immediately, wild horn and fiddle music filled the room.

"Oh, let's dance." Emily put the album cover down and wheeled herself into the middle of the room. She pulled the small levers on either side of her chair forward, locking her rear wheels in place. Then she started clapping her hands, snapping her fingers, and moving her body in time to the music. Lydia joined her, doing a four-step grapevine back and forth in front of Emily.

"Hey, want to do a turn?" Emily asked.

"Sure. Wait a minute." Lydia ran to push all the chairs back against the wall. She threw two big camel-colored pillows that had been lying on the floor out into the hallway. "Do you think there's enough room?"

Emily looked around, released her brakes, and moved her chair across the floor. "I think so," she said, grabbing Lydia's hand. Emily used her free hand to manipulate her wheelchair, and soon she was dipping under Lydia's arm and gliding around to her other side, while Lydia bent her knees and gracefully moved her body.

The song ended, and "*Rozinkes mit Mandlen*" came on. Lydia went to turn the record off, but Emily said, "No, leave it," so Lydia flopped down on the couch instead. Emily wheeled over to sit next to her while they listened to the song. Lydia's eyes grew moist, and she wiped her tears with the back of her hand. "*Nu*, what did I tell you?" she whispered loudly, pointing to her face. Emily took one of Lydia's hands and listened intently to the music until the song was over.

"Did Judy sing that song at the concert?" she asked, as Lydia got up to turn off the stereo.

" 'Raisins and Almonds'? I don't think so."

"It's really familiar. Maybe my grandmother used to sing it to me," Emily said as she watched Lydia slip the album back inside its cover. Lydia put the record away and returned to Emily's side.

"So, are you ready for my song?"

"As ready as I'll ever be."

Lydia opened her notebook and flipped through a few pages. "First I have to explain a few things," she said. "Number one, it's not really a song because I haven't written the music yet. I was kind of hoping Alix Dobkin would do it."

"Uh-huh." Emily nodded her head.

"Em-i-ly." Lydia exaggerated the syllables of Emily's name to illustrate her extreme annoyance.

"What? I didn't say anything."

"Yeah, but you were thinking it."

"What was I thinking, Miss Clairvoyant?"

"You were thinking, 'Alix Dobkin would never waste her time on something as stupid as Lydia Shapiro's Yiddish Lesbian limericks.' "

"You wrote Yiddish lesbian limericks? This I gotta hear."

"Oh shit. Now you made me give it away." Lydia held her notebook up closer to her face. "Listen, they are kind of stupid. I was just trying to use all the Yiddish words I knew, and you know I have a warped sense of humor anyway."

"Yeah, so?"

"So, I was just trying to get the feel of the language. A lot of words rhyme, you know. Like *cheder* and *seder*, *maydl* and *draydl*. . ."

"*Kichel* and pickle." Emily pronounced pickle with a guttural *ch*, making Lydia laugh.

"See what I mean?"

"Yeah." Emily thought for a minute. She loved word games. "How about *latke* and vodka? Or *kvetch* and sketch? Or Etch-A-Sketch?"

"Very funny."

"Boy, are you touchy tonight." Emily scratched her chin and sighed.

"Well, I just don't want you to laugh at me. Someday I really do want to write in Yiddish, or maybe be a translator even. But this," she gestured with her notebook, "is just fooling around."

"Alright. I promise I won't laugh."

"But Emily, you have to laugh. It's funny."

"O.K., O.K. I'll laugh, I won't laugh. Quit stalling already."

"O.K." Lydia took a deep breath and let it out slowly. "It's in two parts, a mother and a daughter, O.K.? It starts with the mother." She held her notebook up in front of her face so she couldn't see Emily, and began to read:

> *Oy*, Morris, have we got *tsuris*.
> Vat can we do *mit* our *tochter* Doris?
>> It's worse than a *Goy*
>> It's not even a boy
> She's in love *mit* the *maydl* Delores.

"Now this is Doris:"
> Mama, Delores is such a *shayna maydl*
> Her *punim's* as smooth as a *knaydl*.
>> Such a *shayna shiksa*
>> Makes me *kvell* in *meyn kishkas*
> *Oy*, I'm spinning from love like a *draydl*.

Emily howled with delight, and thus encouraged, Lydia went on.

The Mama:
> *Oy*, Doris come light the *menorah*.
> We'll *zing* and we'll *tansig* the *hora*.
>> I'll buy you some *tchotchkes*
>> I'll fry you some *latkes*
> If you don't see that Delores no more-a.

Doris:
> Mama, I don't vant to say the *baruches*.
> I vant *meyn hentes* on Delores' *tuchus*.
>> She makes me all *shvitzig*
>> and soft like *gefilte* fishes
> *Oy*, I'll love her from now until *Sukkoth*.

Lydia looked up, grinning wildly. "Now comes the responsive reading," she said.

The Mama:
> *Oy*, Doris, you're worse than a *vildeh chaya*.
> You think Delores is maybe the Messiah?

Doris:
> But Mama, she makes me so *fraylach*.
> Like I've just eaten forty-nine *knaydlach*.

Lydia shifted her weight and held the notebook so Emily could read along with her. "Now comes the 'Mama's Chorus' " she said, and both she and Emily began to read aloud:

> "*Oy, oy, oy, oy*
> She don't vant to know form a boy.
>
> *Oy vay iss mir*
> She won't even wear a brassière.
>
> *Oy, oy, oy vay*
> Why can't she be like Cousin Fay?
>
> *Oy, Gottenyu*
> What is the Mama to do?

Doris:
> *Oy*, Mama don't make such a *futz*
> Just because I don't vant me a *putz*.
> > Last night I had a *cholem*
> > The whole world had *sholom*
> So you see I'm not really a *klutz*.

The Mama:
> *Oy*, Doris, you got such a *shayna smeckle*.
> Maybe you got just a *bisseleh seckle*?
> > Go get me some *lox*
> > I'm ready to *plotz*
> I'm so *fahmished* I feel like a *yekl*.

Lydia turned another page. "*Oy*, there's more?" Emily asked. "*Shah*," Lydia said. "This is Doris."

Mama come sit down and *essen* a bagel.
Nice and fresh they are, from *Tante Raizl*.
   I'll bring Delores to *Shabbos*
   We'll all *shep* some *naches*
It'll be fine, you'll just be amazl.

"Amazl? What kind of *farshtunkeneh* Yiddish is that?" Emily asked.

"Keep *shtil*. Here's the responsive reading again." Lydia turned her head toward Emily to give her a dirty look, then turned back to the notebook again.

The Mama:
   But what if the *Zayde* sits *shiva*?
Doris:
   I'll bribe him *mit shmaltz* and chopped liver.
The Mama:
   And *Bubbe* Esther and Minnie the *Yente*?
Doris:
   Oy their faces like *borsht* so magenta!
The Mama:
   It's the same from Miami Beach to Poughkeepsie.
   The *maydls* go *mit maydls* just like gypsies.
      Vot can we do but say *l'chaim*
   And next year in *Yerushalayim*
   We'll *trink* and we'll *tanse* till we're tipsy.

"I thought Jews didn't drink," Emily whispered loudly.
"Only Manischevitz," Lydia whispered back. "This is Doris:"

See Mama, I'm not such a *shlimazl*.
I'm giving you double *tov-mazel*.
   Instead of *ein tochter*
   You now have *tsvey tichter*
It's even better than Harriet and Ozzl.

Emily cracked up. "Harriet and Ozzl? Oh my God, Lydia." Lydia glared at Emily. "This is the last verse."

The Mama:
   Oy, vat will I do *mit meyn* Morris?
He vanted for you the tailor named Boris.
   We won't have a *chuppa*
   We'll have *kugel* for supper
And then we'll all *zing* in the chorus.

Lydia turned the notebook so Emily could see the words again, and together they read aloud the grand finale:

Oy, oy, oy, oy
Our cup is all filled up *mit* joy.

Oy vay iss mir
The *tochter's* a little bit queer.

Oy, oy, oy vay
The neighbors will give a *gershray*.

Oy, Gottenyu
The Mama will have to make do.

   La la!"

Lydia threw down her notebook triumphantly, jumped up and took a bow with one arm draped across her belly and the other behind her back. Emily applauded wildly, and then put two fingers in her mouth and whistled shrilly.

"Thank you, thank you," Lydia said, taking another bow and throwing kisses at Emily. "So what do you think, Em? Are we talking total fabulosity, or what?" Lydia knelt down in front of Emily and leaned her elbows on the arms of her wheelchair.

"I think you've finally flipped your lid, Lyd," Emily said, ruffling Lydia's short curly hair. "I can't believe my best friend is turning into the Allen Sherman of the lesbian community."

"Well, if not me, who?" Lydia asked.

"I think it's 'If not now, when?' Emily said, correcting Lydia's misquotation of Rabbi Hillel, and still stroking Lydia's head. "It's great, Lydia, really. I love it. I think you should do it at the next lesbian talent show. The girls will go wild."

"Do you really think so?" Lydia sat up, clasped her hands together, turned them inside out and pulled, thus loudly cracking all eight of her knuckles at once, a gesture Emily hated. Emily responded by working up a good supply of saliva with her tongue, opening her mouth wide, and letting a big spit bubble form between her lips.

"Emily, gross!" Lydia looked away.

"Well, you started with your god-awful knuckles."

"Alright, alright, truce." Lydia spread her fingers wide and placed them on her thighs, and Emily closed her mouth. Lydia scooted up and leaned her elbows on Emily's knee.

"You know, Em, it's kid of ironic when you think about it," she said, running her fingers along the cold metal arm of Emily's wheelchair. "I mean, seventy years ago, my grandparents were taking English lessons, and here I am giving myself Yiddish lessons."

"Yeah, it is kind of funny." Emily picked up Lydia's notebook from the couch and turned a few pages, wondering for a minute if Lydia had misspelled *shlimazl*.

Lydia let out a deep sigh. "Em?"

"Yeah?" Emily put the notebook down.

"I'm afraid my grandmother is going to die before I learn Yiddish well enough to talk to her." Lydia got up from the floor, sat down on the couch, and rested her head on Emily's shoulder. "She's really old, you know. All her brothers and sisters are gone. Her whole culture is gone. Just imagine what it would be like to not hear your own language for fifty years." A tear welled up in Lydia's eye.

"I think you should call her up, Lyd, and just talk to her," Emily said softly, stroking Lydia's cheek.

"But what could I say? I can't read her my song."

"You certainly can't." Emily thought for a minute. "Do you know how to say 'I love you, Grandma'?"

"Sure, that's easy. *Ich hob dir libe, Bubbe*."

"Well, you could start with that."

"I guess." Lydia sighed again. "But what if she laughs at me, Emily? Or what if she doesn't understand?"

"She won't laugh, Lydia. And she'll understand. I'll bet you a dozen whole-wheat bagels." Emily smiled. "She'll understand," she repeated.

"You know what, Em?" Lydia took Emily's hand and started playing with her fingers. "What I really want to do is learn Yiddish, and then raise my kid bilingually. Wouldn't that be something?"

"I'll say." Emily stretched her arms high over her head and arched her back. "It just goes to show you, Lydia. The more things change, the more they stay the same."

"Can I quote you on that, *Reb* Emily-*Bat*-Sylvia?

"I expect you to, *Reb* Lydia-*Bat*-Harriet." Emily let out a yawn. "I should get going."

"What, before dessert?"

"What dessert? I'm so full I'm *plotzing.*"

"I cooked a little rice pudding, it shouldn't be a total loss. C'mon, I'll make some decaf." Lydia rose and started for the kitchen.

Emily followed, protesting. "I don't know, Lydia. I really don't think I could eat another thing."

Lydia, who had already put two small bowls on the table, turned around to face Emily, with two teaspoons in her hand.

"But Em, I made it special. I used brown rice and everything."

Emily stopped her chair in the middle of the floor. "Brown rice pudding? *Feh!*" She pretended to spit on the tips of her fingers and then shook her hand at the floor. "What, all of a sudden a health food nut you're turning into?"

Lydia finished filling the coffeemaker with water and then turned to face Emily, a look of astonishment on her face. "But Emily, I thought you wouldn't eat it if I used white rice."

"Hey, bagels are bagels, but rice pudding is rice pudding," Emily said, taking the two mugs Lydia was handing her and putting them on the table. Then Lydia took the big glass bowl of rice pudding out of the refrigerator and set it on the table. A minute later, the decaf gurgled. Lydia poured some into each mug and then sat down across from Emily. The *Shabbos* candles were almost out, but the wicks still flickered above the rim of the brass candlesticks.

"*L'chaim,*" Lydia said, lifting her cup.

"*L'chaim*," Emily answered, raising her own cup and touching it to Lydia's with a clink. Then each woman dipped her spoon into the rice pudding, and first Lydia fed Emily and then Emily fed Lydia, so that they would both have a sweet week until they met again the following Friday night for *Shabbos*.

Sunday Afternoon

"Are you ready to go see Grandma?"

I was sitting at the kitchen table with my father, eating a poppy seed bagel, and reading a story in the *New York Post* about a girl who had been kidnapped by some guy and kept in a cage for eighteen days. Then when they found her, she said she didn't want to go home. She said she had gotten used to being in a cage and she felt safe in it, and well taken care of. At least that's what the article said. Kind of weird, I thought, as I speared another piece of lox with my fork. But the weirdest part was, I kind of knew what she meant.

"Louise?" My father was waiting for an answer.

"I guess so," I said, without much enthusiasm.

"We'll leave in about half an hour, O.K.?"

"O.K.," I answered glumly. Why am I always the lucky one, I thought, as my father sat back in his chair and lifted up the sports section of the *New York Times*. I could just see the top of his salt-and-pepper hair above the black and white newsprint.

How come you don't ask Alice to go, I wanted to say, but I already knew the answer. Your sister has a lot of important things to do, my father would say. She has to get ready for the wedding. The wedding, the wedding, all we ever hear about around here is the wedding. Gross. It's only November and Alice isn't even getting married until June, but every week something else has to be done—the flowers, the invitations, the bridesmaids' gowns. It's all so boring. And the most boring part of all is Jeffrey, Alice's boyfriend. He comes over all the time and my mother makes such a fuss over him, you'd think he was Moses or something. *Jeffrey, sit in that chair, it's much more comfortable. Jeffrey, you want some noodle* kugel? *I just made some special. No don't get up, Louise will get it for you.*

Thank God I'm never getting married, I reminded myself as I bent down to put on my shoes. They were under the kitchen table as usual, and I was glad my mother wasn't around to yell at me about them. She was out somewhere with Alice and Jeffrey for a change. This week I think they were looking at the ushers' tuxedos.

I straightened up and my father put his newspaper down at the same time. "You'll stay with Grandma, while I go visit my brother in the hospital, O.K. Weezie?"

"O.K.," I mumbled, pulling the book review section toward me. My father only calls me Weezie when he wants something from me. My name is Louise, and if that isn't bad enough, I couldn't say my *L*'s when I was a little kid, so I started calling myself Weezie. Of course my parents thought that was adorable, so the name stuck. Alice took it even further and started calling me Weasel, and you can just imagine how I feel about that. I got her back, though, by calling her Lice. She told me if I ever call her Lice in front of Jeffrey, she'll kill me. I'm surprised he hasn't thought of it himself. If I ever get out of here—here meaning my parents' house and high school—I'm gonna tell everyone my name is Lou and just leave it at that.

My father had his elbows propped up on the table and his head bent over the paper, but I could tell he wasn't really reading it. I watched him stare at the same paragraph for a few minutes and I felt kind of sorry for him. "How is Uncle Jacob?" I asked.

"The same," my father answered, without lifting his head. "Poor Jacob. And poor Selma. What that woman hasn't been through." Selma is my Uncle Jacob's wife. Her first husband died of cancer too.

My father closed the sports section, pushed back his chair and stood up with an *oy*. "Louise, will you please clear off the table so your mother doesn't have a fit? Then we'll go." He left the kitchen, taking the magazine section with him, and a minute later I heard the bathroom door close.

After I flipped through the book review section, pretending to be an intellectual, I put the top on the butter dish, closed the cream cheese, and wrapped the *lox* up in its waxed paper. Then I put all the food away, gathered the newspapers together in one neat pile, and carried the dishes over to the sink.

That's another reason I'm never getting married, I thought, as I let the water run. It's always the wife who gets stuck cleaning up everyone else's mess—clearing the table, doing the dishes, sweeping the floor. I rolled up my sleeves and started rinsing out a glass.

I wasn't exactly thrilled about spending the afternoon with my grandmother. We'd drink tea and eat stale Stella D'Oro cookies and she'd ask me at least a million times why I didn't have a boyfriend. You'd think with Alice getting married and all, they'd let up on me a little bit. But no, if anything, that just made things worse. When's the next wedding going to be, everyone always asks. Even the salesgirl at the bridal shop asked me that when she zipped me into my pale blue bridesmaid gown. "Oh, doesn't she look precious?" she'd asked my mother. Precious. Give me a break.

I'm never getting married, I told myself again as I dried off the silverware. I'm going to live all by myself in a cabin by the ocean with a dog and a cat, and everyone will leave me alone so I can draw and paint. That's what I like to do best, and I'm good at it, too. I like to paint the pictures inside of me, like when I'm dreaming, and I like to paint the pictures outside of me, too, like the portrait I did of my best friend Jennifer. Everyone says it looks just like her, and her mother liked it so much, she even paid me ten dollars for it and put it in a frame and hung it in their living room.

My parents aren't wild about the idea of my being an artist. My mother keeps telling me I should take typing and shorthand classes. "You need something to fall back on," she says. "Just in case." What does she know about it anyway? She falls back on my father. My father says no wife of his is going to work. A woman should be at home taking care of the house and the family. And get this—my mother agrees with him. She says why should she go out and work, there's plenty of work to be done right here. Yeah, I sure know what she means, because I'm the one who winds up doing most of it.

I sat back down at the table, scraping the bagel crumbs and a few stray poppy seeds together in a pile with the back of my hand. At exactly 1:00 my father appeared in the kitchen doorway wearing his brown jacket and dangling his car keys.

"Let's go," he said.

I followed him out to the car, and we started driving toward Brooklyn. My father was pretty quiet. I wondered what he was thinking about and figured it was probably Uncle Jacob. I guess I'd be sad, too, if Alice was dying of cancer. I mean, even though I don't like Alice very much, I know I'd feel terrible if something awful like that ever happened to her.

I sighed and looked out the window. My father turned toward me. I could tell because I have this emerald ring I wear on the ring finger of my right hand, and even though I was facing the window, I was really looking into my emerald ring and watching my father's reflection in it. You have to have it at just the right angle. It comes in handy when you want to look at someone and not let them know you're looking at them. I showed Jennifer, and now she can do it, too, in her topaz ring. Topaz is her birthstone. She was born in November just like my mother. Emeralds are for May. I held my fist up to my cheek and watched my father glance over at me a few times. Then he cleared his throat. I knew that meant he had decided to have a conversation with me.

"How's school?" he asked.

"It's O.K." My father always asks me that and I always answer him the same way. He took his right hand off the steering wheel and let it rest on the seat between us. I glanced at his hand and inched a little closer to the door. My father likes to touch me a lot. He's always putting his arm around my shoulder or holding my hand. Alice doesn't seem to mind when he does it to her, but I hate it. Besides, we don't see very much of Alice anymore because she's always out with Jeffrey.

"Did your mother tell you your Cousin *Rivka* is pregnant again?" my father asked.

"Yeah, she told me."

"She's really hoping for a girl this time, but as long as it's healthy, it doesn't matter. Such beautiful boys she has. How old is Stevie now, seven, eight? It's unbelievable how fast the time goes."

I don't know. To me time was going pretty slowly. I had been in high school practically forever, and I was still only in eleventh grade.

"And did you hear your Cousin Richard is getting divorced?"

"Richie's getting divorced again?" In spite of myself, I showed some interest.

"Yeah, he moved out last week into his own apartment. He never should have married that girl. I told him a hundred times I didn't like her. But you know your Cousin Richard, you can't tell him anything." My father looked over his shoulder, sped up and changed lanes. "Listen, don't mention the divorce in front of your grandmother, O.K.?" he said. "I don't want her to get upset."

"O.K." I turned away from him and stared out the window again. Everything was grey and zooming by—cars, trees with bare branches, and brick buildings with lots of windows. It was a really gloomy day. I looked at the man in the car next to us, hunched over his steering wheel. I could have sworn I caught him picking his nose, and even that didn't cheer me up.

Finally we got to Grandma's neighborhood, the neighborhood my father grew up in. All the buildings on my grandmothers's block looked like they were about to crumble. And everything was grey, dirty grey, the sidewalks, the buildings, the sky, as though I was looking at the city through a screen door.

We found a parking space, got out of the car, and started walking up the street. I rammed my fists into my jacket pockets so my father couldn't hold my hand. He took my elbow instead and maneuvered me across the street, toward my grandmother's apartment building. Before we got to the front door though, we were intercepted by Goldie, my grandmother's sister. Nobody in my family likes Goldie very much, though they never say why.

"Murray!" she cried, coming up to us with her arms outstretched. "Murray, how are you? Is this Louise, such a big girl, *kinehora*, she looks just like her mother." Goldie stepped back a little and looked me up and down. I hadn't seen her or any of my relatives for a while, because about a year ago, when Uncle Jacob got sick, we stopped spending the holidays with them.

Goldie finished inspecting me and turned to my father again. "Listen Murray, I gotta talk to you. It's about your mother." Here Goldie raised her hand to partially cover her mouth and lowered her voice so I wouldn't hear. I immediately perked up my ears and pretended not to listen at the same time. It's not as hard as it sounds, really. I just stand there and make my eyes go blank, like I'm not really there, and the people talking aren't there either. Usually it works pretty well.

"Yesterday, or was it Friday? Friday, I think it was. Murray, I went up to have some tea with her. There wasn't a drop of food in the house, Murray. No milk. No bread. Nothing. Not a crumb. She can't take care of herself anymore, *Moishe*. You've got to do something about it." Goldie paused, glanced at me, and lowered her voice even further. "Then, when I left, I picked up her shoes from the middle of the floor, she shouldn't trip and break her hip, God forbid. Holes in them, Murray, all the way through, like someone on welfare."

My father grabbed my arm and pulled me closer to him. "Alright, Goldie, alright, it's enough already. Where is she?"

"She's around the side of the building," Goldie said, half turning in that direction. "Listen, Murray, there's a few more things you should know about. . . ." But my father was already walking toward the side of the building, dragging me along with him, and leaving my Great-Aunt Goldie mumbling in the wind.

When we turned the corner, I saw a bunch of old people huddled together on a bench. I don't know why, but they reminded me of pigeons. It took me a minute to realize that one of them was my grandmother. She looked really old, a lot older than she had looked last year, and kind of shrunken.

"Oh, here's my son," she said, putting one hand on the bench and standing up. Everyone turned in our general direction. "And there's my granddaughter. Hello, *mameleh*." My grandmother always calls me *mameleh*. My father nudged me forward, and I gave my grandmother a hug. She smelled like a musty old attic. "Hi, Gram," I said.

"Hiya Mom." My father bent down and kissed her cheek. "Let's go upstairs."

"What, such a hurry you're in? Alright, alright, my son, he has important things to do," my grandmother explained to the other people on the bench. A few of them nodded.

My father took my grandmother's arm, and she walked slowly in between us around to the front of the building. I was relieved to see that Goldie was nowhere in sight. My grandmother was wearing a scarf around her neck tied under her chin, and a black wool coat, and she carried a big black patent leather pocketbook on her arm. When me and Alice were little she used to keep butterscotch sucking candies in there for us. And she used to keep a little packet of tissues in there, too, and when one of us had a smudge on our face, she'd take out a tissue, spit into it, and rub our skin until it was raw.

We entered the building and while we waited for the elevator, I remembered to look down at my grandmother's shoes. They looked O.K. to me. There were a few old men in the lobby, and Grandma showed us off to them.

"This is *Moishe*, my son, and this is Louise, my granddaughter. Ain't she gorgeous? And this is my friend, Mr. Moskowitz, a very nice man, and this is Mr. Soloman, he lives downstairs."

"Why don't you tell them the truth, Pearl?" Mr. Moskowitz came slowly toward us, shaking a crooked finger at my grandmother. "I'm her sweetheart," he announced when he reached us, placing his cane solidly on the floor.

"Oh go on," my grandmother said, trying not to smile. "Did you ever hear such nonsense in your whole life? Oh, here's the elevator," she said, as the door slid open and we followed her on.

My grandmother lived on the eighteenth floor, which was really the seventeenth floor, because there was no thirteenth floor in the building. As we rode up, I thought about doing a painting called *The Thirteenth Floor*. It would be really creepy, with lots of spooky stuff like spiders and ghosts and skeletons in it. And I'd do it all in black and white, with a little bit of red, for blood.

We got to Grandma's apartment and took off our coats. I was really surprised to see how skinny my grandmother had gotten. The flesh fell from her upper arms like batter dripping from a wooden spoon. She sat down in a green easy chair, and the cushions almost swallowed her up.

"What's this about no food in the house?" my father asked, heading for the kitchen. "I'm going to run an inspection."

"Oh, that sister of mine," Grandma said, putting her small hand on my arm. I was standing next to her chair so I wouldn't have to yell at her from across the room. We were quiet for a few minutes, listening to my father opening cabinet doors and slapping them shut.

Grandma sighed. "*Oy*, such a *yente* she is, always making trouble. She doesn't have a kind bone in her body, *mameleh*, and I'm not ashamed to say it. Everyone in the whole building says so. Two sisters, they say. And so different, like day and night. She's always been like this, a real troublemaker."

My father came out of the kitchen and sat down on the sofa across from my grandmother.

"You gotta eat, Ma," he said, patting the cushion beside him. I crossed the room and sat down next to him. As soon as I leaned back, my father put his arm across my shoulders. Immediately, I sat forward and rested my elbows on my knees.

"I eat, I eat. Look at me, I'm as big as a horse," my grandmother said. Then right away she changed the subject. "Look at her, *Moishe*, such a gorgeous granddaughter you gave me. Ain't she something? The boys must be going crazy over her." My grandmother and my father both stared at me for a minute, and I looked down at the glass candy dish shaped like a heart on my grandmother's coffee table.

"So tell me, *mameleh*, how's school?"

I looked up. "School's fine, Grandma," I said loudly.

"And *nu*, which boy are you going with now? Jeffrey?"

"No Grandma. Jeffrey is Alice's boyfriend."

"*Nu*, where is Alice? Why didn't she come to see me?"

"She's out with Rose, shopping for the wedding," my father answered, crossing his legs.

"So when's the next wedding going to be?" my grandmother asked.

"I don't know, Grandma," I mumbled, tapping my foot impatiently.

"What's the matter, you can't find a boy good enough for you? They're all *shmoes* maybe, like your Cousin Richard?"

I looked over at my father and he looked back at me in surprise. "How'd you hear about Richard, Ma?"

"Hear? I hear, I hear. You think you can keep secrets from a Grandma?" My grandmother leaned forward a little in her chair. "Listen, one night last week I get a funny feeling, I want to talk to Richard. So I call him up, and the wife, that nogoodnik, answers the phone. So where's Richard, I ask her. He's not home, she says. Eight o'clock and he's not home already? So I tell her to tell Richard he should give his grandmother a call. Nine o'clock he doesn't call, ten o'clock he doesn't call. I start to get worried. Maybe he was in an accident, God forbid, maybe something happened. So I call her back, I tell her I can't sleep until I hear from Richard. So what could she do?" My grandmother shrugged her shoulders. "So she tells me."

My father took off his glasses and rubbed both eyes with the fingers of one hand. He always does that when he's tired. "Ma, is there a grocery store around here open on Sundays?"

"What, a store?" My grandmother leaned a little more forward. "Yeah, sure, Waldbaum's is open."

"Good, let's go shopping, we'll get you some food."

"What food? I don't need no food, I'm going tomorrow. You don't have to take me shopping."

"Louise can take you while I go visit Jacob."

At the mention of my Uncle Jacob's name, my grandmother slumped back into her chair. "So how is my *Yacov*?"

"He's O.K., Ma. You want to go see him?"

"Yeah."

"O.K., we'll go. Louise, get my mother's coat." My father stood up and I went to get Grandma's coat out of the closet. I handed it to him, and he buttoned her into it and tied her scarf around her neck as though she were a child.

We didn't say anything as we left Grandma's apartment, rode down the elevator, and made our way back to the car. The day was still grey, like the world had suddenly turned into a black and white television set or something. When we got to the hospital, we circled the building a few times until we found a parking space pretty close to the front door because my grandmother can't walk too far.

Inside, the hospital was teeming with people. It was just about two o'clock, the start of visiting hours, and everywhere I looked people were scurrying around carrying flowers, teddy bears, newspapers, and boxes of candy. Everyone was in a big hurry. When the elevator arrived, there was a mad dash to get on. My father took my elbow and Grandma's arm and drew us back until the crowd thinned out a little bit. We waited until the next elevator opened. Inside it were two men in green pajamas, both of them sitting in wheelchairs.

"Just a minute, just a minute," one of them said, as he tried to maneuver his way around the elevator to make more room. First he tried going forward and then he tried going back, but he only succeeded in getting his leg caught in the other man's chair. "God damn it," he sputtered, trying to back up again. But it was no use because by this time people had pushed into the elevator and he couldn't budge. My father herded us forward, so we got on as well.

"Move back. Move back," some people behind us were yelling. The crowd of visitors surged forward.

"Two wheelchairs, two wheelchairs. No more room," someone said from the back. Someone else pushed a button and the elevator door closed.

"Oh, thank God," a woman in a fur coat said to me. "I almost wound up on that man's lap." We both turned toward the man in the wheelchair who was still sputtering.

"Third floor." "Seventh floor." "Tenth floor." People were yelling again. This day was turning out to be Excedrin Headache #31. My father, who was standing near the door, pressed all the buttons. I noticed that the hospital didn't have a thirteenth floor either.

We got out on the tenth floor and my father told me to stay in the hallway with Grandma. A minute later he appeared in the doorway, beckoning to me impatiently, as though I'd been keeping him waiting.

Make up your mind, I thought, as I took my grandmother's arm. "C'mon Gram," I said, steering her into the room.

It was a large dayroom, filled with men with shaved heads, all wearing baggy green pajamas. It looked like a prison, or rather what I imagine a prison would look like, having never actually been in one. But it couldn't be much worse than this, I thought, as I looked around. To tell you the truth, I was getting a little creeped out. Right in front of me, this guy was slumped over in a chair with his back all humped up, like he'd been in that position for about fifty years. On the other side of the room a bunch of men were watching TV. Some of them sat on couches and some of them were in wheelchairs. One man had a tube coming out of his nose that stopped in mid-air. Another guy had a big red square outlined on his neck. I wondered if it was blood.

I kept looking around the room, holding onto my grandmother and not knowing what to do, until I heard my father call, "Over here."

I looked to my left and there he was, sitting on a couch with some people I didn't recognize. I took my grandmother over there and sat her down in a blue armchair. She melted into it and didn't speak or move for the rest of the afternoon. I got myself a folding chair from a stack against the wall, opened it, and sat down between my father and my grandmother. On the couch next to my father sat a young woman with long blonde hair held back with two gold barrettes, and next to her sat Uncle Jacob.

The grey day outside was absolutely brilliant compared to Uncle Jacob's complexion. He looked faded, like he might disappear at any moment, right in front of our very eyes. I know this sounds sort of cruel, and I should have been thinking how sad it was that Uncle Jacob was dying and all, but to tell you the truth, I was really thinking about how I would paint a portrait of him. His face was a mixture of grey and green, and the skin around his neck fell in spirals that reminded me of the red and white stripes around a barbershop pole. He couldn't have weighed more than seventy pounds, and his bones stuck out everywhere except his feet. Uncle Jacob's feet were swollen to about three times their normal size, and they looked sort of blue. I wondered why he wasn't wearing any socks. His eyes were hazel, just like my father's and my grandmother's, only they had no life in them at all. They sort of looked like mine when I make myself go invisible, except my eyes are a dark brown.

"Is that Louise?" the woman with the blonde hair next to my father asked. She held out her hand to me. "Louise, don't you remember me? I'm your cousin Arlene."

"Oh, hi," I said shaking her hand. I hadn't seen Arlene in a long time, and she sure looked different. She was only a few years older than me, but she looked all grown-up, with high heels and lipstick and everything. I noticed a small engagement ring on her right hand. It was pretty, not huge and gaudy like the obnoxious rock Jeffrey had given Alice.

"*Moishe.*" Uncle Jacob leaned forward toward my father. His voice was high-pitched and shaky. "*Moishe, viffle ha zeyger?*"

My father looked at his watch. "Half past three, *Yacov*," he said softly.

"Half past three? Half an hour it is already and it's not working? *Moishe*, you gotta do something—the shots, they're supposed to work after twenty minutes. Already it's half an hour and they're not working."

"Alright, *Yacov*, calm yourself down. You want me to get a doctor?" My father was already out of his chair.

"*Oy* these doctors, *Moishe*, a bunch of *shlimazls*. One says this, one says that. Meanwhile the pain is eating away at me like a worm in a rotten potato. *Oy oy oy, ich hob nit ken mazel.*" Uncle Jacob let out a long sigh and fished around in his lap for his cigarettes. Slowly he put a Camel between his lips, and then tried to light it. His hands shook, and he went through five matches before he got the thing lit, but nobody tried to help him.

I wondered what drug they had him on. I don't know why, but I had the feeling it was morphine. My father watched his brother for a while, without saying anything. Uncle Jacob smoked peacefully and even relaxed a little in his seat. His eyes looked even more glazed over. I guess the shot was taking effect.

"Excuse me," my cousin Arlene said, standing up abruptly. She brushed off her skirt and raced out of the room, like she couldn't get out of there fast enough. My father watched her go, glanced at Uncle Jacob, and a minute later followed her out.

So there I was, in the land of the living dead, so to speak. I know that's a mean thing to say, but I was really starting to feel kind of weird. My uncle wasn't saying anything, my grandmother wasn't saying anything, and I began to feel like I was in one of those "Twilight Zone" episodes where everyone except the star gets frozen in time. I sure hope I don't get cancer like my uncle, I thought, staring down at his feet. And I sure hope I don't get old and senile like my grandmother, either, I thought, as my eyes traveled to her shoes. I decided I would die by the time I was fifty, but then I got scared. That was only thirty-four years from now, and it didn't seem like such a long time.

To distract myself from such morbid thoughts, I glanced over at the TV, the only moving thing in the room. A football game was on, and every once in a while the men sitting in front of the set would give a half-hearted cheer. I can't tell you how depressed that made me feel. Besides, I couldn't watch the game without seeing the man with the red square on his neck out of the corner of my eye, so I turned away and walked over to the window. The view wasn't all that different from my grandmother's house, or the car window. Buildings, cars, trees, people—all grey. I was beginning to wish I had a pair of rose-colored glasses to see the world through.

I went back to my chair just as my father came back into the room. He talked to Uncle Jacob for a while, and I made my eyes go blank so I could listen. Not that it mattered, though. My uncle hadn't yet noticed that I was sitting there. I guess it had all been too much for Cousin Arlene and she had gone home. I couldn't blame her—I don't think I could stand seeing my father looking like that. Then Uncle Jacob asked my father to bring him a carton of cigarettes next week, and my father said he would, and then they started talking in Yiddish, too fast for me to understand them.

Finally, my father stood up. "Ready to go?" he asked. I nodded. I had been ready all afternoon.

I stood up and side-stepped over to my grandmother. She was still slumped down in her seat, wearing her coat and staring straight ahead of her, at nothing. I touched her gently on the shoulder. "It's time to go, Gram," I said. She didn't respond, so I stood her up and took her arm. My father hooked her other arm through his, and we walked out of the room.

We were quiet in the car on the way back to Grandma's house. The silence was thick, like a plastic bubble, protecting us from the rest of the city. I began to feel drowsy.

"Where's the grocery store, Ma?" my father asked, shattering the silence.

"On the corner of Cropsey and 64th." My grandmother leaned forward and put her arm on the back of the front seat, catching part of my hair. I leaned forward, setting myself free, and for a minute I felt like I was the mother and my father was the husband and my grandmother was the daughter, but then I remembered who everyone was.

When we got to the store, my father tried to make me and my grandmother wait in the car, but Grandma insisted, so we all got out to go shopping. I wheeled a cart slowly up and down the aisles with my grandmother holding my arm and my father taking things off the shelves and putting them into the basket.

"You like grapefruit, Ma?" he asked.

"Yeah, half a grapefruit I like in the morning with a little sugar, it shouldn't be so bitter, you know, *mameleh?*" My father picked out a bag of grapefruits and put them into the cart.

"How about apples?"

"Apples? No, no apples, my teeth ain't that good."

"Bananas, then?"

We continued down the aisles. Soup. Bread. Coffee. And a little story about each one.

"Rice? Yeah, rice is good. *Oy,* how your father used to love my rice pudding, *mameleh.* With raisins I make it, and a little cinnamon." And my father put a box of rice in the cart as we inched our way forward.

The bill came to about thirty dollars, and my grandmother fumbled around in her bag for her change purse. But it was too late. My father had already paid. "*Moishe,* here's some money, take it. Take it," my grandmother insisted, pressing a few bills into his hand.

"Don't be silly, Ma," he said, handing the money back to her. My grandmother looked at me and I shrugged, so she put the money away.

We put the bundles and my grandmother in the back seat of the car and drove to her house. Then me and Grandma waited in the lobby while my father drove around looking for a parking space.

"I never wanted to be a burden, *mameleh,*" she said to me, and I could see her hazel eyes growing moist. "You're not a burden, Grandma," I said, feeling a knot forming in my stomach. Then, since I didn't know what else to do, I took her hand and held it in my own for a moment. I wished I could think of something to say to make her feel better, but I couldn't, so we just stood there, holding hands and waiting.

My father's face appeared in the glass window of the front door. "Oh, here's your father," my grandmother said, hurrying to open the door for him. "*Oy Moishe,* such heavy bundles, let me take one from you, you shouldn't hurt your back." My father handed one of the bags to me over my grandmother's protests and we rode up in the elevator again. When we got back to Grandma's apartment, I put away the food and put up some water for tea.

"Look where everything is Ma, so you'll know," my father said. "The soup here, the rice here, the Ritz crackers on the bottom shelf. What's this?" He had opened up a cabinet full of empty bottles. "What are all these bottles for?"

"What, the jars? They come in handy, *Moishe*. You never know when you're going to need an empty bottle."

"But so many? Throw them out, Louise." I opened a paper bag and filled it, as he handed me bottle after bottle.

The water boiled, and I made tea. My father put some prune-filled Stella D'Oro cookies on a plate and brought them into the living room. We sat down and sipped our tea. My father was the only one who ate anything. The clock on the wall ticked loudly, and I was beginning to feel sleepy again. Then all of a sudden my grandmother leaned forward and pushed away her tea.

"He looks terrible. Why don't they tell me the truth?" She looked first at my father and then at me. "He's dying. A mother knows. A mother can tell. What, you think I don't got no eyes in my head maybe, I don't see my own son shrinking away to nothing? What kind of nogoodnik doctor is taking care of him like this? *Oy vavoy*, that I should live to see such a thing."

"Don't be silly, Ma. He's gonna be fine," my father said, sipping the last of his tea. I scowled at him and looked away. Go on, be silly Grandma, I said to her silently. Stand on your head, tell us a joke, give him the finger. It had been a long day.

"We gotta go now, Ma." My father stood up and collected the tea cups. He brought them into the kitchen and dropped them into the sink with a clatter. Immediately, I went over to wash them.

"Don't forget about the food, O.K., Ma? Call Goldie if you're too tired, she'll come in and cook."

"Goldie? *Oy*, Goldie's cooking I need like a hole in the head." My grandmother got up to kiss us good-bye. "Good-bye, *mameleh*."

"Bye, Gram." I kissed her cheek. It was thin as paper and I felt really sad, like as soon as we walked out the door she would crumble. She held the door open for us, and as I stepped through it, she put her hand on my arm. "*Mameleh*, don't be such a stranger, *eppes*, I'm not getting any younger. *Oy kinehora*, so big you are already. Next time you come you'll bring Alice with you."

"Bye, Mom." My father bent down to kiss her cheek and then we were gone, out the door, through the lobby, down the elevator, and into the street. I was so glad to be going home that I forgot to put my hands in my pockets and before I knew it, my father was holding my right hand, his fingers interlaced through mine. His wedding band rubbed against the silver ring I wear on my pinkie, and it hurt a little. But there was nothing I could do about it now.

The ride home seemed shorter than the ride there, which is kind of strange since they're the exact same distance. It was getting dark, and the sky was a deep royal blue, one of my favorite colors that I use in my paintings a lot. I wondered what my mother was making for supper, and I wondered if Alice and Jeffrey would eat with us. I hoped not. I'd had enough for one day.

"You know, she never said that to me before. I wonder how she knew," my father said softly, almost to himself. She's old, but she's not stupid, I thought, staring at him through the semidarkness. Anyone with half a brain could see that Uncle Jacob was dying. But then, aren't we all?

"Don't be sad, Louise," my father said, as though he had read my mind. He does that every now and then, and it's kind of spooky. "We have to go on. Life's for the living. You gotta do what you gotta do." He pulled off the highway onto our exit, and as we got closer to our house, he began to whistle a little tune. Then he interrupted himself to speak to me again.

"You know what, Louise?" he said. "It's just as easy to be happy as it is to be sad. And whatever happens, I'm gonna be happy."

And whatever happens, I thought, as we pulled into our driveway, I'm going to be sad.

And that, as my grandmother would say, is what makes horse-races.

The Best Revenge

I.

As her childbearing years came screeching to a halt, Gloria Epstein decided to take stock of her life. She flopped down on the couch naked, for it was so hot she had just worked up a sweat by grating a carrot into the potato salad that was now chilling in the refrigerator. She picked up a pen and her journal and started making a list of all she had achieved since arriving on the planet in 1949.

Under WHAT I HAVE, she wrote Good Health. "And if you have your health you have everything," she said aloud, imitating her ninety-nine-year-old grandmother who, thank God, except for thick glasses and a pair of sparkling white dentures, was more or less intact. Under Good Health, Gloria wrote Nice Apartment, Decent Teaching Job (with health insurance for once in my life, she reminded herself), Lots of Books, and Matching Towels. Gloria chewed the end of her pen thoughtfully. "That's it for thirty-seven years?" she asked the newly painted walls. "My health, an apartment, a job, some books, and towels?" She tapped the pen on her notebook and recrossed her legs, which were resting on the old camping trunk she used as a coffee table. "Oh yeah," she said, nodding her head. "I almost forgot—Ellen."

Gloria wrote down ELLEN SILVERMAN in big bubble letters, the kind that merge into each other, and filled them in with thin blue stripes. Then she drew stripes in between the stripes until the letters were a solid blue. She hadn't changed her doodling style since high school.

Strange that Ellen should be the last thing on my list, Gloria mused, scratching a mosquito bite on her thigh. Two years ago, not only would she have been the first thing on the list, she probably would have been the only thing on the list. Who cared about an apartment or a job or health insurance, for chrissakes, when your new lover was so hot you never even left the bedroom anyway, except for an occasional trip to the bathroom, and you called in sick as often as you dared?

It's not that I don't love Ellen, Gloria thought, drawing her name again. It's just that after two years, everything is so predictable. She knew how Ellen looked in the morning, with her straight brown hair smushed against one side of her face and the ends all sticking up like a ruffled bird. She knew what Ellen liked for breakfast: pecan spice granola with a plop of vanilla honey yogurt. Ellen had eaten that same breakfast every morning Gloria had woken up with her for the past two years. "Hey, I'm into cereal monogamy," she'd said, when Gloria teased her about it. She even knew the way Ellen liked to be touched, with two fingers inside her vagina and Gloria's thumb massaging her clitoris in a circular motion (counterclockwise was best).

There was no doubt about it. They were definitely growing stale. Gloria wrote STALE under Ellen's name and started filling in the letters with little blue dots. They had hardly had any sex in the past six months. I bet I could count the times on the fingers of one hand, Gloria thought, starting a new list: How Many Times Ellen and I Have Done It Since March. Let's see. There was that time after Jackie's birthday party when we kissed a little, but then Ellen said she was too tired and had to get up early the next day for work. That doesn't count. Then there was that Sunday morning when we started doing it, but then the phone rang and it was Ellen's brother calling from Pittsburgh. After talking to him she said she wasn't in the mood. Gloria's forehead was beginning to gather in little folds between her eyebrows. She picked up her pen again and started drawing women's symbols down the margin of the page. There was that time when we housesat in July at Bev and Joanne's house in the country, she thought, and we did it outside on their front lawn. That was really nice, except for the end when the dogs started barking because the gasman was pulling into the driveway and we had to run into the house.

Gloria held up her pinkie. "Once," she said to the avocado plant sunning itself on the windowsill. "Not twice, not three times, not eight times, or God forbid 127 times, but once. O-N-E. One." She shrugged her shoulders. "But who's counting, right?" Gloria sighed. She and Ellen were well on their way to becoming a Typical Lesbian Couple, the kind they had read about in one of those lesbian sex manuals, complete with pictures, diagrams, and horrifying statistics: Lesbian couples have less sex than either gay male couples or heterosexual couples. After one to two years, the Typical Lesbian Couple has sex once or twice a month.

"Once a month?" Gloria had gasped, looking up at Ellen. "*Vay iss mir.*" They had been snuggling on this very couch, with Ellen's arm around Gloria's shoulder and Gloria's head resting on Ellen's chest.

"Don't you worry your pretty little *kepeleh* about it," Ellen had answered, kissing the crown of Gloria's head. "That'll never happen to us."

"It better not," Gloria mumbled, nuzzling her face into Ellen's breasts.

"Hey, what are you doing down there?" Ellen murmured, as Gloria's mouth encircled her breast over her thin cotton T-shirt.

"Just fighting statistics," Gloria had answered, letting her tongue lick Ellen's hardened nipple, and that was all it had taken to get them started. They'd made love right there on the living room floor.

Those were the days, Gloria thought, her cunt wet from the memory. She thought about masturbating, but it was just too hot. She turned to the next page of her journal and started a grocery list. She hadn't been to the store since last Tuesday, and her cupboard was beginning to look like Old Mother Hubbard's. Let's see. Milk, eggs, bread, carrots, celery, tuna fish, cat food, spaghetti sauce, granola and yogurt for Ellen—the same damn thing every week. Clearly, Gloria was bored. When the grocery list takes priority over masturbating, she thought, running her hands through her curly brown hair, something is definitely wrong.

She threw down the pen and paper, pushed herself up from the couch, and walked into her bedroom, shutting the door behind her. Even though she lived alone and knew Ellen was at karate and wasn't coming over until 8:00, she still wanted a sense of privacy.

Gloria lay down and reached under the bed for her favorite toy—a large black feather. Ellen used to spend hours running it lightly over her body, smiling and teasing her until she could hardly stand it. Now the feather was covered with dustballs. Gloria cleaned it off and ran it across her nipples, back and forth, back and forth. Instantly they became hard. "You poor little breasts," she cooed to them. "Nobody's paid attention to you for a long, long time, have they?" Gloria spoke to her own body as if it were a child. "You're a good girl, yes you are. Yes. Yes." She took her time, touching her breasts and belly softly, then letting her fingers trace her wetness around and around. Soon her breathing deepened, and she touched herself faster and harder. One hand pinched her right nipple and the other one massaged her cunt until she was just on the verge of coming. I want Ellen, she thought, and her body shook as she came and started to cry at the same time. "I want Ellen. Why doesn't she want me?" Gloria asked the empty room. She wiped her eyes on the purple pillowcase that had a picture of a big black cat staring at a full moon on it. "Suzie Q, I need you," Gloria said, pulling an old teddy bear with one eye missing close to her and burying her face in its fur. She had had Suzie Q since she was seven. "You'll always be on my list, Suzie Q. You're nicer than Ellen." Gloria stuck her thumb in her mouth and stared at Suzie Q's matted fur until her eyes drooped and she drifted into sleep.

Ellen opened the front door, pulled it shut behind her and thrust her keys into the pocket of her jeans. "Glory?" she called, stepping into the kitchen. No answer. That was strange. They had an 8:00 date and it was 8:15 by Ellen's watch. Usually Gloria would be standing in the kitchen by now with that If-You-Really-Loved-Me-You'd-Be-On-Time look in her eyes.

Ellen opened the refrigerator and took a swig of iced tea out of the blue plastic pitcher on the top shelf. Gloria hated when she did that, but Gloria wasn't around, so why dirty a glass she'd just have to wash later?

Ellen put the iced tea back and shut the refrigerator. Scotch-taped to the door was a handmade calendar with the words HAVE YOU CRIED TODAY written across the top. Today was August 10. Gloria had put her initials on August 1, August 4, and August 9. Ellen shook her head with one corner of her mouth pointing down. Gloria and her lists. Ellen was surprised she didn't have one in the bathroom to check off brushing her teeth and washing behind her ears.

She wandered into the living room, thinking maybe Gloria had left a note for her, and noticed Gloria's bedroom door was shut. That was also strange.

"Glor?" Ellen opened the door a crack. "Are you asleep?"

"Yeah," Gloria mumbled, opening her eyes. "What time is it?"

"About quarter after eight. You sick or something?"

"No, just tired." Gloria stretched her arms over her head and held them out to Ellen. "Come give me a hug."

"Nah. I'm too sweaty from karate." Ellen crossed the bedroom and stood in front of the window looking out. "It must be ninety-five degrees in here." She opened the window and propped it up with a stick. "Hey, they're doing some job on that house next door."

"You don't have to tell me. They start every morning at 6:30." The house next door to Gloria's had burned down last February, and already it was halfway rebuilt. Gloria put her arms down and stared at Ellen's profile. She doesn't look so sweaty to me, she thought, her bottom lip beginning to curl. And besides, being sweaty wouldn't have stopped her last summer. Gloria almost said the words out loud, but she knew they'd just start a fight. Instead she flung back the sheet and started fanning herself with the back of her hand. Her therapist had told her to say joining phrases, not contrary ones, when she was talking to Ellen.

"You're right, it is hot in here. I've been *shvitzing* all day." Gloria lifted her hair off the back of her neck. "Are you hungry? I've got some potato salad in the fridge. I thought we could just have that and sandwiches."

"Great. I'm starving." Ellen turned from the window and faced Gloria. "Wanna eat now and then go for a walk?"

"How about an appetizer first?" Gloria asked, patting the bed beside her.

"No thanks. I'm not that hungry." Ellen stared out the window again. "Maybe we should go to a movie. At least it would be air conditioned."

Gloria picked up Suzie Q and mumbled softly into her ear, "Maybe I should just take a cold shower." She was embarrassed that part of her had actually thought the sight of her naked body would make Ellen want her the way she used to. Why, a year and a half ago, if Ellen had come home from karate and found me naked in bed, she would have jumped right on top of me, work boots and all, even if it was 110 in the shade. Hot-shmot, I'm sick of her excuses.

Gloria massaged the space between her eyebrows. C'mon Ellen, don't you want to do it just once, for old times' sake, she wanted to ask. Let's just give it the old college try.

You're asking for trouble, a voice inside Gloria's head warned her. You start with the wisecracks and you know where you'll wind up. You better lay off. Can't you see she's in a rotten mood?

What about me, Gloria wanted to scream. It's always take care of Ellen, Ellen's in a rotten mood. Don't say what I need or think or feel because Ellen will get mad, she's in a rotten mood. She's always in a rotten mood. I'm sick of it.

What kind of lover are you anyway? the voice asked Gloria. Ellen needs to not be sexual because she's dealing with her incest, and all you can think about are your needs.

Gloria sighed and got out of bed. She arched her back and twisted sideways, hearing her vertebrae crack. Look at this gorgeous *zaftig* body going to waste. I'm in the prime of my life, she thought, putting her hands on her hips and admiring her firm breasts. Why, there are dozens of girls who would give their right arm just to have me. But no, I have to be stuck with *her*.

She turned to look at Ellen who was still staring out the window. "What are you thinking?"

"Oh, I don't know. Mostly about my muffler and how much it's going to cost me to fix it." Ellen turned from the window. "I'm gonna set the table. You gonna get dressed or what?"

"Yeah, yeah, I'm coming." Gloria opened her dresser drawer and pulled out a T-shirt and a pair of cut-off shorts. God, we're worse than an old married couple, she thought, zipping up her fly. I'm standing here naked, in all my glory, and all she can think about is her fucking muffler. Jesus. She threw her T-shirt over her head, shoved her dresser drawer shut, and walked into the kitchen.

Ellen had set the table with two plates, two cups, two forks, and two napkins. She had also taken out the bowl of potato salad and the pitcher of iced tea.

"Gloria, do you think your lousy landlord will ever put a screen door in here? These flies are driving me crazy." Ellen lifted a fly swatter off a nail on the wall where it was hanging and started following a fly around the room.

"Oh, I don't know. Maybe someday," Gloria answered, getting out some bread, cheese, and mayonnaise, and setting them on the table.

Ellen swatted the kitchen counter. A split second later she heard the buzz of the fly. "Damn," she murmured. "If it just lands one more time. . . ." She turned slowly, waiting for the fly to stand still.

"Let me try," Gloria said, taking the swatter from Ellen. She slammed the wall, the table, and the windowsill all in vain. "Oh, let the poor thing live in peace," she said, hanging the fly swatter back on its nail. "Let's eat."

They sat down, and Gloria poured out the iced tea. As she was slicing some cheese for their sandwiches, the fly landed on Ellen's napkin. A second later, Ellen's fist slammed down, squashing it flat.

"Alright! I got it! Way to go, Ellen." Ellen blew on her fist like John Wayne cooling off his pistol.

"You killed it," Gloria said, the cheese slicer in mid-air. "I can't believe you did that."

"Gloria, for God's sake, it was only a fly." Ellen scooped up the dead fly in her napkin, and got up to throw it away. "Anyway, you were trying to kill it too."

"Yeah, but I knew I wouldn't get it."

"Oh, come on."

"I did." All of a sudden Gloria's chin began to tremble, and a tear welled up in her eye. "All life is sacred, you know. It could have been a reincarnation of your Grandma Minnie, or Barbara Deming, or . . .Gertrude Stein!"

"Gloria, oh my God, is the heat getting to you or what? Listen, if that fly was Gertrude Stein, she'll thank me in another lifetime for putting her out of her misery. I'm sure Gertrude Stein wouldn't want to be a fly stuck in some dyke's funky apartment on Maple Street in August."

"It's not that bad!" Gloria's voice was rising. "What if her next reincarnation is being a spider plant, and she has to hang under a florescent light in a Howard Johnson's somewhere, watching people licking their stupid ice cream cones for the next fifty years? You think she'd like that any better? Huh?"

Ellen helped herself to a big glob of potato salad. "Glory, will you listen to yourself? You sound like you're losing your mind."

"I am losing my mind!" Gloria shrieked, scraping back her chair. The tears were flowing freely now. Usually Gloria didn't cry in front of Ellen since Ellen never cried and hated when anyone else did. But she was too upset to control herself. "This is what happens when your lover doesn't touch you for six months. You do start losing your mind."

Ellen slammed down her fork. "Oh my God. Does everything have to do with that? Even a fucking fly? Gloria, you have a one track mind. You're just like my father."

"I am not your father!" Gloria was yelling now, and she didn't care. "I did not rape you. You are not six years old. You chose to be in a sexual relationship with me out of your own free will and, as I recall, you used to like it. I'm taking some space." She ran into her bedroom and slammed the door.

Oh shit. Ellen put a forkful of potato salad into her mouth and chewed thoughtfully. Gloria will kill me if I just sit here and finish dinner. She sighed, not knowing what to do. Doesn't she know it bothers me just as much as her that we haven't had sex in six months? Doesn't she think I'm a little concerned?

If only Gloria was an incest survivor, then she'd understand, Ellen thought, resting her chin on her fist. Immediately she felt guilty. "Goddess, cancel that. I didn't mean it," Ellen said, raising her eyes to the ceiling. "I wouldn't wish incest on my worst enemy, let alone my lover." Ellen picked at the potato salad on her plate. But it isn't fair. She can choose to walk away anytime, and then she'll never have to deal with being a six-year-old playing "Let's Wash Daddy's Thing in the Bathtub and Watch It Grow." She can just walk away. I'm stuck for life. It isn't fair.

The thought of Gloria walking out of her life made Ellen's stomach turn. Gloria was the best thing that had ever happened to her. Ellen still remembered the night they met, two summers ago at a women's dance. Ellen had been standing by the pool table, waiting for her name to come up, when this gorgeous woman in a black tank top and white pants came over and stood a little ways away from her, leaning against the wall in a very deliberately casual manner. Every time Ellen glanced over at her, Gloria would quickly look away. When Gloria got up the nerve to glance again at Ellen, Ellen would look away. It was a definite sign of mutual interest. Ellen had played pretty well that night, all the while conscious of the way her shirt fell open when she leaned over to shoot, exposing the top part of her tan breasts. Ellen had been hoping that Gloria was conscious of it, too.

After she lost the pool table, Ellen went to return her cue stick to the rack, managing to smile at Gloria as she passed. "Nice game," Gloria said, and then blushed because Ellen had lost. "I mean, it doesn't matter if you win or lose, it's how you play the game, right?" Ellen had watched as Gloria's blush deepened and spread across her face. "Oh hell, since I've made an ass out of myself anyway, wanna dance?"

It's always the femme that makes the first move, Ellen thought, as Gloria took her hand and led her onto the dance floor. They danced easily together, each sneaking shy looks at the movements of the other's body. Then a slow number came on, and by the end of the song, Ellen knew where she'd be spending the night.

Another fly buzzed against the window, bringing Ellen back to the present. She knew she should go knock on Gloria's door, take her in her arms and comfort her. And maybe she would. But first she wanted a few more minutes of peace and quiet.

Ellen crossed the room and took the fly swatter down from the wall. All she and Gloria seemed to do was fight these days. In some ways it felt the same as the early days when they fucked all the time. Well, they do say that anger and arousal come from the same part of the brain, Ellen thought, tapping the swatter against her hand. And the body goes through similar changes: your heartbeat quickens, your blood runs faster, your skin flushes.

She sat down at the table again, remembering the first time they had made love—right here in this very apartment, in the very bedroom where Gloria was now doing God-knows-what. Ellen had been amazed at how a red flush had spread all across Gloria's face, down her neck and across her breasts. It was just like the dawn spreading across the sky. "You're my blushing bride," Ellen had crooned to her, stroking her flesh which was hot to the touch. "I want to make you hot all over." And she did, all night long.

We sure were something, Ellen thought, pushing back her chair and standing up. She walked through the apartment and knocked on Gloria's door.

"Gloria?"

"Yeah?"

"Can I come in?"

"Yeah."

Ellen opened the door to find Gloria sitting at her desk with one leg crossed over the other. "What are you doing?"

"Making a list."

Oy vay, Gloria and her lists. "Can I see it?"

"Maybe." Gloria looked down at the piece of paper and scratched something out. "It's called CHOICES FOR ME AND ELLEN."

Ellen sat down on the edge of Gloria's bed and clasped her hands over her knees. "Will you read it to me?"

"Yeah." Gloria rubbed her eyes. They always swelled up after she cried. "CHOICES FOR ME AND ELLEN. One: break up. Two: don't break up. Three: become nonmonogamous. Four: stay monogamous. Five: change Ellen so she wants to have sex. Six: change Gloria so she doesn't want to have sex. I couldn't think of anything else. Can you?" Gloria looked up at Ellen.

"How about none of the above?" Ellen dropped her head into her hands and stared at a splotch of white paint on the toe of her left workboot.

"What do you mean?" Gloria asked, putting her pen down.

"I don't know." Ellen didn't look up. "I don't want to break up with you, and you know I can't handle nonmonogamy. I just wish things could be like they were before."

"You do?" Gloria swiveled around in her chair and leaned forward, resting her elbows on her knees until her head was level with Ellen's. Now they were both staring at Ellen's workboots. "You never told me that. I thought you just hated sex." Gloria raised her eyes and stared at the crown of Ellen's head. She wanted to reach over and stroke her hair, but she didn't dare.

Oh, Ellen, sex is no big deal, she wanted to say. An orgasm is just an orgasm. I just want to be with you. But if she said that, she knew

Ellen would never let her forget it and then they'd never have sex again and then Ellen would get bored and leave her. So she remained silent.

"I don't hate sex. Goddess, of all people, you should know that." Ellen looked up into Gloria's eyes and then looked down again. Actually, she didn't care one way or the other whether they had sex or not. But if she told Gloria that, Gloria would say, "If you don't care, let's just do it," and then they'd be having sex all the time again, and she didn't want it to be like that. She wanted Gloria to love her for other things, too.

They remained silent for a while, each lost in her own thoughts. Finally Gloria got off her chair and sat down next to Ellen on the bed. She put her arm around her and started stroking her back up and down.

"It's always the femme," Ellen mumbled to her shoe, smiling in spite of herself.

"Yep. It always is. Ellen, sit up. Look at me." Ellen sat up slowly and looked into Gloria's eyes. "Ellen, I love you. I want to be with you. But I can't stand all this fighting and distancing and the way you're so hard with me. I feel like I'm being rejected all the time."

"Gloria, I'm not rejecting you. I just don't want to be sexual right now."

"That's bullshit."

"No it's not."

"Yes it is." Gloria started to cry again, and she wiped away her tears impatiently with the back of her hand. "Yes it is," she repeated. "If I was pretty enough and good enough, you'd still want me. I know you would."

"Do you really believe that?" Ellen was surprised.

"Yes, I do." Gloria wiped her nose on her T-shirt. "There has to be something wrong with me. Otherwise you'd still want me."

"Gloria, come here. Come here honey." Ellen took Gloria in her arms and brushed the tears from her eyes, and that simple act of tenderness made Gloria cry even harder. Ellen stroked her back and rocked her.

"Ellen, I'm so scared you're going to leave me. I don't know what to do." Gloria gasped between her sobs. "I'm so afraid you don't love me anymore. I miss you." She buried her face in Ellen's chest.

"Me leave you?" Ellen stroked Gloria's hair. "I've been scared you're going to leave me. I don't want to break up, Gloria." Her voice became soft. "I don't want to break up, Glory. I don't." After a minute she added, "I miss you, too."

"But what about sex?" Gloria spoke into Ellen's chest. "I want to have sex with you."

"I know you do, honey."

"We used to have sex all the time, Ellen, and you used to like it." Gloria's voice was pleading now. "Didn't you?"

"Yeah, I liked it." Ellen let out a deep breath and stared over Gloria's shoulder at a smudge mark on the wall. How could she explain to Gloria what she didn't understand herself—that she always had lots of sex in the beginning of a relationship in order to win someone over, and then after a year or so she closed up tight as a clam? I know it has something to do with my incest, Ellen thought, but Gloria will never understand. She just thinks I don't want her anymore. "Yeah, I liked it," she repeated.

"But now you don't anymore," Gloria said dully. She wanted to shake Ellen, crack the hard shell that had grown around her and set the old Ellen free. Actually, Gloria missed this more than she missed sex, this hugging and stroking and cuddling that Ellen had long denied her. But since any kind of touching had always led to making love, Gloria had no words to express this, even to herself. She sighed. Sometimes she thought it would be much easier if they just stayed girlfriends but never had sex again.

She leaned her weight against Ellen and shut her eyes as Ellen continued touching her—rubbing her back, brushing her hair away from her face, stroking her thighs. It felt so good just to be caressed like this. It was almost enough.

Ellen felt Gloria's body relaxing in her arms and something stirred inside her. Feelings of tenderness and compassion swept over her, feelings for Gloria she hadn't felt in a long time. She almost wanted to kiss her. She did in fact want to kiss her, but she was scared. What if Gloria gets mad and pushes me away, Ellen thought, feeling tiny beads of sweat collecting on her forehead. Or, what if she responds and then I freak out and push her away? I can't win. A tear slid quietly down Ellen's cheek. I want to give Gloria what she wants, but I can't. I'm too scared. But what if we never have sex again?

Another tear leaked out of Ellen's eye. My heart hurts, she thought, feeling a tightening in her chest. I want my mommy. Where is she? I need someone to take care of me.

"Gloria, I'll be right back," Ellen said abruptly, sitting up and pushing her away.

"Where are you going?" Gloria asked, looking up in surprise to catch a glimpse of Ellen's back leaving the room. She had been just about to ask Ellen if she wanted a massage, or a back rub, even though she was scared she wouldn't be able to do it right.

"I just need a drink of water." Ellen stepped through the living room and into the kitchen, her tears blurring the half-eaten dinner still on the table. A feeling of panic was rising from the pit of Ellen's stomach, up through her throat, threatening to strangle her. I've got to get out of here, she thought, as the walls started closing in.

She opened the front door and paused for a minute, as though she had forgotten something. Quickly she walked over to the refrigerator, took a pen out of her breast pocket and wrote her initials in the square marked August 10 on the HAVE YOU CRIED TODAY chart. Then she ran out of the kitchen, not hearing Gloria burst into tears at the sound of the front door slamming shut, for her ears were full of the sound of her own sobs: the sobs of six-year-old Ellen and the sobs of thirty-four-year-old Ellen, all mixed together in one tremendous howl.

II.

Gloria pulled into Sandy's driveway and beeped the horn twice with the heel of her hand. It was one of those rare New England summer days—hot and dry with the sky as clear and sharp as glass. Gloria was glad she was going swimming with Sandy, instead of sitting in the house feeling sorry for herself. She lifted her eyes to the rearview mirror and met her own reflection. Cheer up, kid, she told herself. Things can always get worse.

"Hi, gorgeous." Sandy spread her towel out on the front seat, sat down on top of it, and leaned over to give Gloria a kiss. "Where are you taking me?"

"How about the Quarry?"

"Sounds good." Sandy threw her knapsack over her shoulder into the back seat and buckled her seatbelt as Gloria backed out of the driveway and headed for the highway.

"Oh, I'm exhausted," Sandy said, letting out a big yawn. "All this doing nothing tires a girl out, ya know? It almost makes teaching bearable."

"Yeah," Gloria mumbled, without turning her head. She seemed to be preoccupied with something, and Sandy knew it wasn't her driving.

"Hey, why the long face?" she asked, turning in her seat so she could face Gloria. "Here you are on a gorgeous day, going to the Quarry with your best friend—who by the way also happens to be gorgeous—what more could you want?"

Sex, Gloria thought, as she rammed the stickshift into fourth. Aloud she said, "I'm just in a pissy mood because me and Ellen had a fight last night."

"Uh-oh." Sandy leaned her arm along the back of the front seat. "What was this one about?"

"A fly."

"A fly," Sandy repeated, tilting her head to one side. "You mean the kind you unzip?"

"I wish." Gloria looked over her shoulder and pulled into the passing lane. "No, the kind that buzzes around, you know, as in 'I wish I could have been a fly on that wall'." She put her blinker on and steered back into the right lane, in front of the station wagon that had been slowing them down.

"So you fought about a fly, huh? Well, at least you two are getting more creative."

"Oh Sandy, we fought about sex again and it was awful."

"I had a feeling." Sandy reached over and started massaging Gloria's right shoulder, which was slowly creeping up toward her ear. "How the hell did a fly lead to sex?"

"I don't know. Everything leads to sex these days. Or to no sex is more like it. Sandy, can you believe that me and Ellen have had sex once in the last six months?"

"Big deal. I've had sex once in the last six years."

"But you don't have a girlfriend."

"Don't remind me."

"Anyway, you're exaggerating. It hasn't been six years. It's been what—two, three?"

Sandy folded her arms as Gloria turned off the highway. "Three years, nine months and twenty-seven days," she said, staring out the window.

"Well, part of the time's been your choice. You didn't want a girl-friend, remember?" Gloria made a left turn onto a dirt road and pulled over to the side. "We're here."

They got out of the car, slung their knapsacks over their shoulders, and headed down the dirt road walking together easily, side by side. Gloria and Sandy were the same age, and they had known each other since their late twenties when they were the only out lesbians in grad school. They had spotted each other immediately: Gloria had been tipped off to Sandy by her short buzz-cut hair and her full breasts that were obviously braless under her Medusa T-shirt. Sandy had recognized Gloria as one of her own by the more subtle silver labyris hanging around her neck from a purple string.

They had seen each other through a lot over the past ten years: new jobs, new apartments, the death of Sandy's fifteen-year-old cat, the trauma of Gloria coming out to her parents, and, of course, the various lovers that had come and gone in and out of each other's apartments and lives. For the last few years, though, Sandy had been single by choice, a choice Gloria didn't really understand. "I'm being my own lover for a while," Sandy had explained, as she indulged herself in solitary candlelight dinners, long luxurious yarrow baths, buying little presents, and even writing love letters to herself and dropping them in the mail. Gloria thought it all a little strange, like having a make-believe friend when you were a kid, but she never said much about it. After all, Sandy was her best friend, and God knows, Gloria had her own quirks.

They turned off the dirt road onto a path that cut through the trees and came out onto a wide stream surrounded by flat rocks big enough to lie down on. There was one rock in particular that Gloria and Sandy had dubbed their own. It was big enough for two, shaped like a pear cut in half lengthwise, and on bright sunny days like these, drenched in sunlight for most of the afternoon. They headed for it now.

"This is great," Sandy said, spreading out her towel and stepping out of her clothes. Gloria did the same. The Quarry was deserted, as it usually was on weekdays, except for a few squashed beer cans and an empty pack of cigarettes wedged between two rocks.

"Umm, the sun feels good." Gloria lay down flat on her back and shut her eyes. "This always reminds me of high school when me and Lindsey used to lie in the back yard and work on our tans. We lay flat on our backs like this," Gloria spread her fingers out, making sure not one inch of her body was in the shade, "for half an hour. I used to bring my alarm clock out, can you believe it? Then we'd roll over on our bellies for fifteen minutes with our left cheeks down," Gloria rolled over and turned her head, "and for fifteen minutes with our right cheeks down. God forbid we should have uneven cheeks."

"That would be a disaster," Sandy said, lying on her side, propped up on her elbows.

"I used to cheat though," Gloria said, sitting up and hugging her knees. "When Lindsey had her eyes closed, I used to turn my head so I could stare at her. God she was beautiful. She had perfect breasts and a tiny waist and long smooth thighs. She was everything I wanted to be."

"You just wanted to get into her pants, you little dyke." Sandy squinted up at Gloria.

"You're probably right. I still do. Who cares if she's married and has three kids, a station wagon, and a VCR? Maybe I should break up with Ellen and try to find her anyway."

"Gloria." Sandy shook her head. "C'mon now. Let's hear about this fight."

"There's not much to tell." Gloria rested her chin on her knees. "I wanted sex, Ellen didn't, she said I was just like her father, I got mad, she left. My advice to you," Gloria added after a minute, "is don't get involved with an incest survivor." She started picking at the fraying edge of her towel.

"That's a shitty thing to say." Sandy shook her head in disapproval.

"I know, I know," Gloria said, looking into Sandy's eyes. "Some of my best friends are incest survivors."

"Gloria!"

"O.K., O.K., I'm sorry. It was just a joke."

"Well, it wasn't very funny."

"You're right." Gloria reached over and stroked Sandy's hair. "Do you forgive me?"

"Yeah. Just don't let it happen again."

"O.K." Gloria paused, staring at the cracks in the rock. "Sandy, do you think I'm a horrible person because I want Ellen to have sex with me?"

"No, of course not." Sandy waved her hand at a mosquito on her leg. "But I don't think Ellen's a horrible person either because she's saying no."

Gloria sighed. "Hey, whose side are you on, anyway?"

"I'm on both your sides."

"I know. You're good."

"Ellen's going through some really hard stuff right now. You have to have some patience."

"I'd rather have some Sarah," Gloria said, stretching out her legs and leaning back on her elbows. "I've been patient for six months. What good is having a girlfriend if you never even have sex? I might as well be single."

"Yeah, you should try it sometime. There are some really good things about it."

"Like what?"

"Like getting to hear all the intimate details of your friends' love lives so you don't have to make the same mistakes they do." She grinned.

"Am I boring you?"

"Oh, no," Sandy said, opening her mouth wide into a big fake yawn. "Though I do have to admit, I have heard this scenario once or twice before." Sandy turned her head to watch a dragonfly flitting over the water. Then she turned back to Gloria. "Did it ever occur to you that maybe you don't need sex right now? Maybe you need to learn how to be intimate in other ways. You know, they say you don't always get what you want but you do always get what you need."

Gloria groaned. Sandy had recently joined a woman's meditation and spirituality group, and she was always sprinkling their conversations with these weird slogans. "Well, I'm definitely not get-

ting what I want, I'll give you that. But how do I know I'm getting
what I need?"

"You don't have to know. The Goddess will provide."

"*Oy vay* Sandy, you sound like a Jesus freak."

"I'm just trying to help." Sandy sat up and wiped her sweaty forehead with the edge of her towel. "When Allie and I decided to be
celibate for a month, it was one of the best times we had together."

"What'd you do the whole time, play poker?"

Sandy ignored Gloria's sarcasm. "We found other ways to be
intimate."

"Like what?"

"Oh, like giving each other back rubs, holding each other, reading stories together, going for long walks." Sandy traced Allie's name
on the surface of the rock with her finger. Even though breaking
up had been the right thing to do, she still missed her after three-
and-a-half years. "You know, if Ellen knew you two were going to
spend time together that wasn't sexual, she might be more open
to spending time together that was."

Gloria scooted over to the edge of the rock and stuck her feet in
the water. She stared down at her cold wet toes. "It's always up to
her," she grumbled. "The whole lousy relationship is on her terms."

"Well, when you're an incest survivor, it's important to have some
control. Especially around sex. Besides, what do you care whose
idea it is, as long as you're getting what you want?"

"But I'm not getting what I want." Gloria kicked her foot in the
water, sending a splash of drops flying.

Sandy sat up, unzipped her knapsack, and pulled out the latest
issue of *Woman Of Power.* "Gloria, Ellen's a fine woman. You're
lucky to have her. Look, lots of incest survivors go through a time
when they don't want sex. It's part of the healing. Ellen will get
over it."

"How?"

"I don't know how, Glor. Everyone's different." Sandy opened her
magazine. "Listen, why don't you try not bringing up sex for a
while, like a month maybe, and see what happens?"

"A month!" Gloria pulled her feet out of the water.

"Yeah, a month. You'd be surprised at what can happen when
the pressure's off."

"Not with Ellen. She'd be happy if the subject never came up again." Gloria folded her arms and her breasts fell naturally into her hands. She squeezed them twice for reassurance. God, another month! By then the whole summer will be over, and I'll be back at school with a million papers to grade every night. We'll never have time for sex. Aloud she said, "I don't know, Sandy. If I just let it drop, that'll be the end of it."

"I'd give Ellen a little more credit than that." Sandy scanned the table of contents. "Don't you think Ellen's upset too? I'm sure she's in a lot more pain about this than you are."

"Now you're taking her side." Gloria stood up and turned her back to Sandy.

"Well, if you want to know the truth, it sounds to me like you want sex more than you want Ellen."

"That's not true!" Gloria stamped her foot and turned around.

"Then why can't you just leave her alone for now?"

"Because I'm not perfect, O.K.? Because I'm not little-miss-wonderful-girlfriend who can say, 'Sure, honey, it's O.K., I can wait thirty years until you work it out. I'll just jerk off until the year 2000, don't you worry about me.' "

Sandy turned to an article on "Sports and Visualization." "I think you should break up with her, Glory, and find yourself a red hot mama. Sounds like that's what you want."

"No. I want Ellen." Gloria paused, watching Sandy study a picture of a woman lifting weights. "But I want sex, too."

"Well, you can't have both," Sandy said, looking up. "Today, anyway. And you've got to make up your mind."

"I have made up my mind. I'm going swimming."

"Good idea. You need some cooling off." Sandy shaded her eyes with the back of her hand and started reading her magazine.

Gloria slid her body into the cool water and swam over to a little alcove where there was a deep pool surrounded by rocks that formed little ledges around the water. She leaned back on one of the rocks and watched the sun reflecting on the water. It was so quiet and peaceful here. She loved the way the water felt tickling her body. The way she was leaning caused her breasts to float up to the surface, and the cold water made her nipples hard. Almost without thinking, Gloria's left hand crept toward her cunt. She glanced over at Sandy who was absorbed in her magazine. She can't see me under the water anyway, Gloria thought, as she slipped two fingers inside. She just kept her hand there, not bringing herself to orgasm, but just feeling quiet within herself. It helped her to think.

Maybe Sandy's right. Maybe I am just a sex maniac. Gloria watched an orange butterfly opening and closing her wings on a nearby rock. Maybe I should let go and Ellen will come around. Then again, maybe she'll just break up with me. Who knows? I do like sex, she thought, but it's not more important to me than Ellen. As Gloria stared at the moving orange wings, she remembered that corny saying, or was it a song, about chasing butterflies: the more you ran after them, the more they flew away, but if you sat very still, one might come and land on your shoulder.

"C'mon. C'mon," she whispered to the butterfly, extending her hand. But the sound of her arm moving through the water was enough to send the butterfly on her way through the trees. Was that an omen that Ellen was going to fly away from her? Discouraged, Gloria swam back toward Sandy, who was now lying flat on her belly with her eyes closed.

Gloria climbed out onto the rock and wrapped herself in her towel.

She stood with the sun behind her, so that her shadow fell across Sandy's back. When she didn't stir, Gloria bent over and shook her wet hair, sprinkling Sandy's long smooth back with icy cold drops.

"Hey!" Sandy rolled over and sat up.

"Sorry. I couldn't resist." Gloria squatted down on the rock and dried her face with the edge of her towel. The smell of her cunt on her fingers drifted up her nostrils. She hoped the scent wasn't drifting up Sandy's nostrils, too.

"Sandy?"

"Umm?"

"Can I ask you something?"

"You just did."

"Wise guy." Gloria rocked back and forth on her heels. "Sandy?"

"Umm?"

Gloria pulled the towel more tightly around her. With her unruly brown curls and her body coiled into a ball like that she looked just like a little girl. Sandy watched her and waited.

"Sandy, do you think me and Ellen will ever have sex again?"

"I don't know, Gloria. But leaving her alone would probably help."

"But I'm too scared." Gloria's voice burst out of her throat. "I just feel so desperate these days, Sandy, you know, like if Ellen doesn't have sex with me soon, I'll die." Gloria looked up at Sandy and there were tears in her eyes. "You know, half the time when we're fighting about it, I don't even want sex. I don't know what I want. But I just push and *nudge* until one of us gets really mad and the whole night is ruined, and then I'm satisfied. And I know I'm doing it the whole time, too, and I just can't stop myself." Gloria sighed and looked down. "Sandy, don't you think I'm an awful person?"

"No." Sandy scooted over until she was right next to Gloria and put her arm around her. "Listen, it's O.K. You and Ellen picked each other for very good reasons. You'll work it out."

"But what should I do?"

"Well, Doctor Sandy prescribes cutting out sex, even talking about it, for one month. That'll be fifty dollars." She held out her hand.

Gloria wasn't about to be cheered up so easily. "I can't, Sandy, I'm too scared."

"Well, how about a week then?"

"Maybe I can do that." Suddenly her face brightened. "How about I promise I won't bring it up tonight?"

"Gloria, you're not seeing Ellen tonight."

"Oh yeah, I forgot. O.K., a week then."

"That's my girl. I knew you had it in you. Wanna go? I'm getting cold."

"Yeah." Gloria stood up and stepped into her shorts. Sandy got dressed too.

"Hey, Sandy, thanks for listening to all that. You're a real pal."

"Hey, no problem. Besides, I've got a lot invested in your relationship."

"You do?"

"Yeah." Sandy put her magazine into her knapsack and zipped it shut. "I can't afford to pull you through another breakup. School starts in three weeks, and I haven't done any lesson plans yet."

"Thanks a lot." Gloria reached down and splashed some water at Sandy's feet. Sandy squatted down, filled her cupped hands and threw the water at Gloria, getting her thighs all wet.

"Truce, truce!" Sandy put her hands up as Gloria threatened to push her into the water.

"O.K., I'll let you go this time, but only because I want to get home."

"You're all heart, pal. C'mon, I'll race you." Sandy took off and Gloria followed, laughing and breathless all the way up the path.

III.

"*Ichi, ni, san, shi, go.*"* The *Sensei*'s voice counted out as crisply as the snap of the women's *gi* pants, as ten left legs kicked out and snapped back in perfect unison. A drop of sweat trickled down Ellen's forehead. She looked neither to the right nor to the left as she waited for the *Sensei*'s next command.

"Twelve *shuri* punches," the *Sensei* ordered, reading from a slip of paper she had tucked into her black belt. "From right where you are. I want you to imagine an attacker in front of you and think about your targets. Full speed and power."

Ellen stood stock still, her back leg straight but not locked, her front leg bent with her knee out over her toes, her right arm out in a loose cover, and her left fist pulled back by her hip in chamber position. She knew who her attacker would be. It was always her father, standing in front of her with that stupid grin on his face. *We've got a special secret, you and me*, he always used to say to her, his words coming from some dark place behind that grin. *Nobody else can know. Just Daddy and Ellie Belly. Because Mommy wouldn't like it and we don't want Mommy to get mad, do we?* Ellen clenched her fist so tightly she started getting a cramp in her arm. Breathe, she told herself. Breathe all the way down into your center. The deeper she breathed, the more angry Ellen got. Some women felt guilty about how much anger they had inside them, but not Ellen. She would gladly beat her father to a pulp, and she did so regularly every Tuesday and Thursday night in karate.

"*Seiken.*" Solar plexus, Ellen thought as her fist shot out. "*Tate.*" Solar plexus again. "*Age ken.*" Rising punch. Groin up to chin.

---

*The italicized Japanese words in this section relate to the practice of karate.

"*Mae-washi ken.*" Side of the head. As the Sensei called out the punches, Ellen imagined bruising her father's body, the body she knew so well, even better perhaps than her own.

They did the twelve *shuri* punches on the other side and then the *Sensei* looked up at the clock. "Two minute water break. Get your gear on."

Ellen groaned inwardly as she lined up at the water fountain with the other women. Even though she'd been training for over two years, Ellen still disliked fighting. What is she going to make us do tonight, Ellen wondered, as she tightened her blue belt. I hope it's not multiple attackers or street fighting. She got a drink of water and then ran to the dressing room to get her gear. She pulled on knee pads, foot and shin guards and gloves, and stood waiting with the other women, her mouth guard wrapped in a blue bandanna on the floor behind her.

The *Sensei* switched on a tape recorder. Soft, slow Japanese flute music filled the air. "Find a partner. Slow sparring. If you think you're going as slow as you can, slow it down even more. Like you're moving through water."

Ellen turned to the woman next to her and bowed. They both stepped back, fists raised, waiting for the command to begin.

"*Hajime,*" the *Sensei* said, and the women started executing techniques in slow motion. This isn't too bad, Ellen thought, keeping her eyes fixed on her partner's throat. It's almost like dancing.

After three minutes the *Sensei* switched off the music. "Find a new partner," she said. Ellen bowed to her partner and turned around to face another woman. They bowed to each other and then stepped back into fighting stance.

"Harmony sparring. Remember, harmony means working with each other, not against each other. Begin." The *Sensei* switched on the music and Ellen and her partner circled each other. Her partner was also a blue belt, so it didn't matter which one of them threw a technique first. Ellen executed a roundhouse kick; her partner blocked it, and stepping to the side managed to get her in the ribs with an uppercut. Since they were moving pretty slowly and using light contact, Ellen didn't worry about blocking her partner's techniques as much as she concentrated on getting her kicks and strikes in. The *Sensei* walked around making comments to her stu-

dents. "Nice. That's it. Go for the openings," she said to Ellen's partner. "That's good," she said to Ellen after watching them for another
minute. "Don't forget to breathe."

They continued harmony sparring for another ten minutes,
switching partners two more times. Then the *Sensei* switched off
the music and said, "Susan, Amy, and Ellen, roll out the mat."

Oh no, not the mat, Ellen thought, running to do as she was told.
That meant street fighting, probably. She and the other two wom-
en rolled out a big rubber mat, covering the smooth polished wood-
en floor. Ellen looked at the clock that hung over the full-length
mirrors covering one entire wall of the *dojo*. Ten after seven. Twenty
more minutes. Anything could happen. She ran to get her mouth
guard and tucked it in under her belt.

"I want everyone to lie down on her back with her knees bent,"
the *Sensei* said. "We're going to practice getting someone off us.
It looks like this." The *Sensei* lay down while everyone watched her.
"You thrust your hips and turn to the side in one motion." The *Sen-
sei* demonstrated a few times, then sat up. "Any questions?" No
one spoke. "Remember, the source of your power is in your hips.
Ready?" Everyone got down on the mat. "On the count. *Ichi. Ni.
San. Shi....*"

Ellen clenched her buttocks and thrust her hips up and over to
the side at every count. This isn't too bad, she said to herself. Maybe
we'll just practice these until class is over.

"Get a partner," the *Sensei* said, dashing Ellen's hopes. "I want
one of you on your back with your knees up, and the other one sitting on top of her, straddling her hips. Now, when I give the count,
execute that technique and get her off you. Attackers, be convinc-
ing. Don't just roll off willingly. Make her push you off."

A woman with a green belt nodded to Ellen, and they bowed to
each other. Then the higher ranking woman lay down and Ellen
straddled her. "*Ichi.*" The woman thrust her hips and sent Ellen
flying over her head. "*Ni.*" Ellen climbed back on, and she did it
again. After ten times the partners switched roles. Ellen lay down
on her back. On the count, she thrust her hips and twisted, causing her partner to lose her balance and tumble off her. Wow, Ellen
thought, it really works.

"Now, I want you to try it by starting with your legs straight, so you're lying flat on your back, with your arms overhead. Attackers, I want you to pin the defenders by their wrists. Same hip motion. Ready?"

Ellen and her partner got into position and took turns practicing. After they had done it ten times, the *Sensei* spoke again.

"Switch partners." Ellen looked around and nodded to the woman standing next to her, wearing a yellow belt. They bowed to each other and waited.

"Now, half of you lie down flat on your backs." Ellen, being the higher rank got down on the mat. "You're going to start with your eyes closed. When you feel your attacker on top of you, I want you to get her off you as quickly as possible and counter with at least three strikes. Remember, go for the primary targets—the eyes, throat, and knees. Attackers, you don't move until I give the signal." Ellen looked up and saw her attacker standing over her.

"All right defenders. Shut your eyes. You're nice and relaxed, you're falling asleep in your own bed, having a nice dream." Ellen let her head flop to one side and her muscles relax as the *Sensei*'s words washed over her. "Just relax. Breathe deeply. Nice deep breaths." Ellen let out a yawn and watched the colors forming patterns behind her eyelids. When she was a kid, she called it Ellen's Wonderful World of Color, after the "Walt Disney Show" that came on every Sunday night after "Lassie."

Ellen was unaware of the *Sensei*'s nod. All of a sudden her attacker was on top of her, pinning her arms over her head. It's only my Daddy, Ellen thought, squeezing her eyes shut even tighter. He loves me. It's O.K.

The woman on top of Ellen was puzzled by Ellen's lack of movement, but she stayed where she was.

If I don't open my eyes, Ellen thought, scarcely breathing, he'll go away soon. I have to stay very, very still. If I don't move at all, sometimes I can disappear.

"Ellen!" The *Sensei*'s voice cut sharply through the air. Ellen's eyes flew open. Everyone else had done the exercise and was watching her. Ellen looked up into the woman's eyes. They were dark brown, just like her father's. She shut her eyes again. I want to see the colors, she thought. Red and yellow and blue and green.

The *Sensei* stared at the two women on the floor. This wasn't like Ellen at all. The woman with the yellow belt looked up at the *Sensei* wondering what to do.

"Get up, Ellen, get up!" The *Sensei* shouted, motioning the other women to do likewise. "Get up, Ellen!" "C'mon Ellen, you can do it." "Use your voice, Ellen. Yell. *Kiai!*"

Ellen's eyes opened once more, and again she saw her father's face above her. A growl like a lion's escaped from her throat. "Grrrr!" She twisted her hips violently, sending her attacker sprawling. Then she crawled toward her punching and kicking wildly, her techniques ending just a few inches from her attacker's body. She rose and continued punching and kicking with all her might as the woman curled up into a ball to protect herself. Ellen's techniques were swift and sure; a hammer fist to the head, an elbow strike to the kidneys, a kick to the knee. Not once, though, did she touch the woman's body. Finally Ellen backed away, keeping her arms up for cover. Then she dropped her hands and the woman stood up and faced Ellen. At the *Sensei*'s command, they bowed.

The *Sensei* looked up at the clock. It was 7:35. "Circle up," she said, walking to the middle of the room. Everyone followed, including Ellen who felt slightly dazed, as though she were indeed moving through water. The women made a circle and stood in *haichi dachi*, ready position.

"Present your left fist," the *Sensei* said. Ten left fists sliced the air. "Has anyone here ever played 'Who's the Boss?' " A few women around the circle nodded. "All right, if you've never played before, follow Marcia and Amy's lead. Ready?" The *Sensei* looked around the circle to make sure everyone's stance was solid and their wrists straight. "Who's the boss?"

"Me!" Marcia and Amy shouted, pulling their left fists back into chamber and punching the air with their right.

"Who's the boss?"

"Me!" Everyone else followed suit.

"Good. Let me really hear you." The *Sensei* got into stance and put her fist out as well.

"Who's the boss of my emotions?"

"Me!"

"Who's the boss of my thoughts?"

"Me!"

"Who's the boss of my actions?"

"Me!"

"Who's the boss of my sexuality?"

My father, Ellen thought, as she threw a half-hearted punch and her chin began to tremble. Her action didn't go unnoticed, though. The *Sensei* was keeping a close watch on Ellen, making sure she was all right. She knew something deep had come up for her during that last exercise, and since many of her students had a history of sexual abuse, she wasn't surprised that this was it.

"Who's the boss of your sexuality?" she repeated, trying to catch Ellen's eye.

"Me!" nine voices yelled.

"Who's the boss of Ellen's sexuality?" the *Sensei* shouted.

"Ellen!" the women answered.

"Who?"

"Ellen!" they shouted, punching the air.

"Who's the boss of Ellen's sexuality?"

"Ellen! Ellen! Ellen!" They screamed her name and punched the air ten times. Ellen punched, too, letting the tears stream from her eyes as her name got bigger and bigger until it filled the entire room. In the silence that followed, she looked up and silently thanked the *Sensei* with her eyes. After the two women stared at each other for half a minute, the *Sensei* spoke sharply. "Kneel for meditation circle." Everyone stepped forward with their right foot, lowered themselves onto their left knee, and sat back down on their heels.

The *Sensei* spoke softly now. "Shut your eyes and think of one positive thing that you achieved today in class. If you can't think of anything else, remember you did get yourself to the *dojo*." After a few minutes she asked the students to open their eyes and relax. "Any questions or comments?" She looked around, but no one spoke. Ellen felt like they were all waiting for her to speak, but she didn't want to start crying again so she remained silent.

"Rise." The *Sensei* lifted her palms to the ceiling, motioning for everyone to stand. "*Orei.*" They bowed their heads thanking the teacher, "*Aragato, Sensei,*" to which the *Sensei* replied, "*Aragato.*" Then Ellen made a beeline to the dressing room, changed her clothes, and ran out into the welcoming arms of the night.

IV.

Ellen climbed into her truck, slammed the door, and started the engine, groaning at the noise it made. Damn, I have to do something about that muffler, she thought, as she pulled out of the parking lot and headed toward Gloria's apartment. Even though they hadn't spoken since their fight Tuesday night, Ellen assumed their standing Thursday night date was still on. A year ago they had come up with a schedule that seemed to work: Gloria would cook dinner Tuesday and Thursday nights after karate class, and Ellen would fix meals on the weekends. At least I'll go over there and apologize for walking out, Ellen thought, as she waited at a red light. She felt exhausted, spaced out, and terrific, all at the same time.

Ellen's the boss, she thought, as the light turned green. She made a right onto Lewis Street and a left onto Maple. "Who's the boss of this truck? Ellen," she said, as she parked in Gloria's driveway. "Who's the boss of these feet? Ellen," she said loudly, as she walked up the steps. "Who's the boss of these keys? Ellen," she said, putting her copy of Gloria's key into the lock and opening the door.

"Hi."

"Hi." Gloria was standing at the stove stirring something in a wok.

"You expecting someone?"

"Yeah, my girlfriend. Wanna sit down and wait with me until she gets here?"

"Sure." Ellen sat down at the kitchen table which was set with two bowls, two glasses, and two pairs of chopsticks. She gulped the ice water in one of the glasses and watched Gloria add some tamari to the food she was making.

"What'cha cooking?"

"Stir fries and tofu. My girlfriend likes to eat kind of light after karate."

"Oh yeah? Is she nice, this girlfriend of yours?"

"Yeah, she's pretty nice. And very cute. Only she's late a lot of the time, and that makes me mad."

"Wait, I think I hear footsteps. I'll go see if that's her." Ellen got up from the table and went out the door. A second later she was back.

"Hi, honey, I'm home," she called.

"Hi. Sit down, you silly goose. Dinner's ready."

"Great. I'm starving. Hey, who was that other woman who just ran out of your apartment?"

"What other woman?"

"Oh, you know, she was tall and had straight brown hair and was wearing jeans and a white T-shirt."

"I don't know, but it sounds like the same woman that ran out of here the other night. Was she crying?" Gloria moved toward the table to get the bowls.

"I don't think so." Ellen refilled her water glass and waited until Gloria finished serving the food and sat down. "Glory, I'm really sorry about the other night. I just lost it, that's all, and I had to leave."

"That's O.K." Gloria picked up her chopsticks. Just before Ellen had come over, Gloria had called Sandy for a little pep talk. Sandy said she was not allowed to pick a fight, criticize, nag, or bring up sex. She was also supposed to show Ellen she was interested in who she was as a human being. After they had gotten off the phone, Gloria had made a list of things she could ask Ellen about: work, her truck, her childhood, karate. "So how was class?" she asked, placing a piece of broccoli into her mouth.

"It was great. We did some really neat streetfighting." Ellen didn't feel like going into detail about class. Not now anyway. What had happened was a secret she wanted to savor, at least for a while. Besides, Gloria was acting a little weird. It wasn't like her to gloss over a fight like that. Usually she made Ellen apologize up and down and sideways, and even if she stood on her head, it was barely enough. Ellen was suspicious. Maybe she's made up her mind to break up with me and she doesn't care anymore. Cautiously she asked, "What did you do today?"

"Not much. Looked over some teaching stuff, went shopping, cleaned the house. I can't believe school starts in a few weeks."

"Yeah." Ellen turned her attention to her food. "This is good."

"Thanks." Gloria looked out the window for a minute, watching a squirrel run up a tree. "So, uh, Ellen, how was work today?"

"The usual. Pretty boring. Want some more water?"

"No thanks."

Ellen got up and refilled her glass. They continued eating in silence until Gloria spoke again.

"So, how's your truck?"

Ellen stared at Gloria in disbelief. How's my truck, she thought, shaking her head slightly. It's parked in the driveway. Why don't you go downstairs and ask it? Aloud she said, "It's O.K., but I've got to get that muffler fixed."

Gloria stared out the window again. So much for conversation. She could always ask Ellen about her childhood, but she was afraid she'd bring up her father and that might lead to you-know-what, so she said nothing.

They finished their dinner, and Gloria went into the living room to relax while Ellen did the dishes. When she put the tamari away, Ellen noticed Gloria had drawn a heart around her initials on the HAVE YOU CRIED TODAY chart. That was a little reassuring.

Ellen went into the living room and sat down on the couch next to Gloria, who had her feet up on the coffee table and the newspaper spread across her lap.

"Want to go to a late movie?" she asked, scanning the entertainment pages.

"Not really." Ellen rested her arm along the back of the couch so her fingers were just inches away from Gloria's shoulder.

"Want to go for a walk then?" Gloria closed the paper and let it slide onto the floor. Ellen's hand began stroking Gloria's shoulder. She twisted her fingers gently through Gloria's hair. "No, I just want to stay here with you."

Boy, Ellen's sure acting strange, Gloria thought, watching her out of the corner of her eye. Why is she being so nice to me? Ellen was now massaging the back of Gloria's neck with strong, sure fingers. Instead of relaxing, though, Gloria felt herself growing more and more tense. Maybe she's going to break up with me, Gloria thought, recrossing her legs. That's why she's being so nice. Because she knows soon she'll be free.

"So what should we do?"

"Let's just talk," Ellen said, tucking a strand of Gloria's hair behind her ear.

"O.K., fine, we'll talk. What should we talk about, the weather? It was another beautiful day here in New England, folks, partly sunny, or was it partly cloudy, anyway it was partly something. O.K., so, moving right along now, we'll talk about, how about the news?

Let's see." Gloria picked up the newspaper. Whenever she was nervous she began talking compulsively, hardly pausing to breathe. It was as though nothing frightening or painful could get to her as long as her words took up all the available space. "Here's an interesting item. Sidney Hennessey of West Springs, Illinois, ate 157 snails in five minutes, breaking the world's record formerly held by John Brockton of Clearview, Tennessee."

"Gloria."

"No, really, it says so, right here in the paper. They have a contest every year, see?" She held the paper up so Ellen could see the picture.

"Honey, I really don't care." Ellen's voice was kind but firm. Gloria read the newspaper religiously and therefore had a wealth of useless information. This made her a great Trivial Pursuit partner and conflict avoider. At the drop of a hat, whenever Gloria felt threatened, she'd shift into what she called her "*shtick* mode," which in addition to the news and weather, consisted of television commercials, top-40 hits, and Broadway show tunes. Sometimes Ellen found this trait of Gloria's endearing, but not at times like these. She took Gloria's hand. "Honey, I want to be serious."

Uh-oh. Gloria looked at Ellen who was staring down at her hand, tracing the shape of her thin blue veins with her index finger. Gloria had that same feeling in the pit of her stomach she used to get when she was called down to the principal's office for wearing her skirt too short, or for clapping the erasers over her math teacher's chair. The princi*pal* is your *pal*, she reminded herself. Aloud she said, "Ellen, if you're going to break up with me, do it now so I can still get to a 9:30 movie." Her voice sounded so distant, that for a minute Gloria thought it was coming from someone else.

"Break up with you? Gloria, I don't want to break up with you, you silly goose. I want to make up with you." She paused, gripping Gloria's hand more tightly. "As a matter of fact, I want to talk about our sex life."

What sex life? Gloria thought bitterly. But she stopped herself from saying it and just waited.

Ellen looked down at the floor. "Well, I've been thinking about it a lot since Tuesday, and I've decided there's something definitely wrong with our sex life."

"This you just realized?" Gloria sat forward on the couch. "Ladies and Gentlemen, a stroke of genius has just descended upon our own Ellen Silverman's head. Mark it on your calendar, folks, August 12, 1986, Ellen Silverman realizes that after six months of no sex something is, and I quote, Ladies and Gentlemen, definitely wrong."

"Will you stop?" Ellen glared at her. "This isn't easy for me, you know, and your acting like an asshole doesn't help."

"I am not an asshole."

"I didn't say you were an asshole. I said you were acting like an asshole."

"It's the same thing."

"No it's not. You're behaving like an asshole, but that doesn't mean that you are an asshole."

"Yes it does."

"All right then, you're an asshole."

"No I'm not!"

"Oh my God, Glory, will you listen to me?" Ellen leaned forward and cupped her head in her hands. This wasn't turning out the way she had planned it at all. She tried again. "Gloria, I'm willing to work on our sex life, but I have to go slow, O.K.?"

Gloria was staring at the hangnail on her left thumb. We had a fight, she thought, frowning. I promised Sandy we wouldn't fight and we did. Ellen was watching her, waiting for her to say something. "What?"

"I said I was willing to try to be sexual. But I have to go slow."

"Oh." Boy, everything changes, Gloria thought. "But I can't."

"Why not?"

"Because I promised Sandy I wouldn't try to make you have sex with me for a month."

"You did?" Ellen's eyebrows rose in astonishment.

"Well, not a month. A week. But after that I was going to try another week, and then another one after that."

"You were going to do that for me?" Ellen asked, taking Gloria's hand. "But you like sex so much."

"Well, yeah, but other things are important, too, you know."

"Yeah, but I didn't think that you knew."

"I do so know. I even made a list. Wanna see?"

Ellen shrugged. "Do I have a choice?"

"Wait here." Gloria went into her bedroom and got her journal. She sat back down on the couch next to Ellen and turned to her latest entry: THINGS I LIKE TO DO WITH ELLEN.

"Here. Read it."

Ellen took the notebook and began to read out loud. "THINGS I LIKE TO DO WITH ELLEN. One: wake up in the morning. Two: eat breakfast. Three: kiss good-bye (if it's a workday). Four: go back to bed and snuggle (if it's not a workday). Five: take a walk. Six: go to the movies. Seven: eat lunch. Eight: eat dinner. Nine: I'm not allowed to say. Ten: fall asleep." Ellen looked up from the notebook. "This is the best list you ever made."

"You like it? Even number nine?"

"Yeah. Especially number nine."

"There's more." Gloria took the notebook from Ellen and turned the page. "Here's another list I want you to read." She handed it back to her.

"THINGS I LIKE ABOUT ELLEN," Ellen read out loud. "When did you write this?"

"Yesterday. Wait, I want to read it to you." She grabbed the notebook out of Ellen's hands. "THINGS I LIKE ABOUT ELLEN. One: her smile. Two: her strong hands. Three: the way she walks with her hands in her pockets and her toes pointing out. Four: the way she shoots pool. Five: the way she eats. Six:. . ."

"The way I eat?"

"Yes, don't interrupt. Six: the way she dances. Seven: the way she holds me when I cry. Eight: her intelligence. Nine: her sense of humor. Ten: the way she's secretly pleased with herself."

Ellen smiled. "You think so, huh?"

"Yeah, I do." Gloria put down the notebook. "Do you like your lists?"

"Yeah."

"You can have a copy of them if you want."

"O.K." Ellen looked at Gloria as though she were seeing her for the first time. She reached out and Gloria took her hand, but Ellen shook it free. "No, I don't want you. I want your notebook and a pen."

"What for?"

"I'm going to make a list."

"You are?" Gloria stared at the stranger who had been her lover for over two years. "What's it called?"

"It's called, 'WHAT I LIKE ABOUT HAVING SEX WITH GLORIA.'"

"Oh my God."

"Be quiet. I'm trying to think," Ellen said as she wrote the title down. "One: how she blushes from her head down to her feet. Two: the way her tongue feels in my mouth. Three: the way I can put both her nipples in my mouth at once. Four: the way I can suck her breast and she can suck my breast at the same time." Ellen looked up from the notebook pleased to see Gloria blushing. "Let's see. Five: the sounds she makes. Six: how sometimes I can't tell whether I'm touching her or touching me. Seven: how wet she gets. Eight: how big she opens up. Nine: how tight she holds me when she comes. Ten: everything else." Ellen finished writing and put the notebook down. "What do you think of your list?"

"It's the best list ever." Gloria spoke in a little voice. "Can I sit on your lap?"

"Sure." Ellen patted her thighs and Gloria climbed on top of them. She rested her head on Ellen's chest and let Ellen rock her back and forth.

"You really like all those things about me?" Gloria asked.

"Yes, I do," Ellen stroked her hair.

"And you really want to you-know-what with me again?"

"Uh-huh."

Gloria thought for a minute. "But what do you mean about going slow?"

Ellen lifted her head so she could look into her eyes. "I just have to make sure I stay present, so I know it's really you, O.K.? You know, sometimes when you touch me, or ask me to touch you, it feels like I'm a little kid again with my father."

"I hate your father," Gloria said, crinkling up her nose. "He's yucky."

"Yeah. But I'm going to get even. You know what my revenge is going to be?"

"No, what?"

"Guess."

"Cutting off his balls?"

"No."

"Cutting off his balls and poking out his eyes?"

"No."

"Hmm. What else could it be?" Gloria scratched her head. "I know. How about cutting off his balls, poking out his eyes, and making him eat 157 snails in five minutes?"

Ellen laughed. "Close, but no cigar." She put her arms around Gloria, held her close, and whispered in her ear. "The best revenge would be having the most fantastic sex life you could possibly imagine with the woman I love."

"Wow," Gloria turned her head to face Ellen. "And who might that lucky girl be?"

"You, you silly old bear."

"Moi?" Gloria poked herself in the chest with her index finger. "Little old moi?"

"Yes, you. You with the big eyes and pretty lips and wild curly hair." She looked at her and grinned.

"So *nu*, what are we waiting for, the Rabbi's blessing? Kiss me."

"No, you kiss me."

"No, you kiss me."

"*Oy*, even this we're going to fight about?" Ellen shook her head. "Only me and you."

"That's right, kiddo. Me and you." Gloria poked her own chest and then Ellen's. "A match made in heaven. I say we continue this fight in the bedroom."

"I knew I should have brought my sparring gear," Ellen murmured.

"Wouldn't you rather have a silk scarf, or a black feather, perhaps?" Gloria whispered, running her hands up and down Ellen's body and stopping at her breasts which were just dying to be released from her tight T-shirt. "C'mon baby," Gloria whispered, letting her tongue roam around Ellen's ear. "Let's strike while the iron's hot."

Ellen turned her head and grabbed Gloria's lips with her own, kissing her with a fierce tenderness. Gloria wrapped her arms around Ellen, holding her tight. Suddenly Ellen jerked away.

"Listen."

Gloria sat up and cocked her head. "What, I don't hear anything."

Ellen put her fingers to her lips. "Shhh," she said. "It's a fly."

"So?"

"So maybe it's my Grandma Minnie, may she rest in peace. I can't do this in front of her."

Gloria nodded her head. "You're right. She'd *plotz*. C'mon." She hopped off Ellen's lap and led her by the hand into the bedroom where the possibilities were as endless and varied as the stars.

Flashback

If no one tells your story, you die twice.
Andrea Hairston, *Signs Of Life*

The first time it happened, Sharon was getting her hair cut. It was on a Tuesday, about four o'clock. She remembered this because she'd had to leave her favorite class, Literature of Despair, a little early in order to make her appointment, and she hadn't wanted to leave because they were discussing her favorite author, Elie Wiesel. But Joshua, the guy who was going to cut her hair, had a very tight schedule, and according to Sharon's best friend Abbie, he was the only hairdresser in town who really understood Jewish hair. And for ten dollars less than the shop price, he'd come to your house, as long as you paid him cash. Sharon wasn't wild about the idea of having a strange man come to her house, but ten dollars was ten dollars, and besides, she had to admit Abbie's hair did look good.

Sharon got home at five minutes to four, dumped all her books on the kitchen table, which was already full of books, papers, and other trappings of student life, and went into the bathroom to consult the mirror one last time. Maybe I'll let him cut it really short, she thought, holding the curly black ends away from her face. After all, summer is coming. So is the end of the semester, she reminded herself, as she hurried past the mess in the kitchen to answer the door. She had no idea how she was going to get all her schoolwork done and find a summer job in one month's time.

Joshua was very brisk. He sat Sharon down in the middle of her kitchen, tied a red plastic smock around her neck, sprayed her hair with a plant spritzer, and immediately set to work with his comb, brush, and scissors. He was gone in less than twenty minutes, leaving Sharon with a shorn head and a tangle of wet curls all over the floor. She stood in front of the bathroom mirror again, studying herself in a mild state of shock. I know I said short, but this is really short, she thought, pulling the ends this way and that. Her head seemed lighter, and she could feel the early evening air at the back of her neck. Oh well, there's nothing I can do about it now, she thought, shutting the bathroom light. It'll grow back. At least no one will mistake me for being straight. Sharon got her broom and dustpan from the hall closet and started sweeping up the black curls that were scattered across the kitchen floor. And that's when it happened.

She had gathered all the hair into one neat pile, amazed that there was so much of it, for her hair hadn't been that long to begin with, and she was just bending over to sweep it into her copper-colored dustpan, when a wave of nausea hit her so suddenly and so strongly that it almost knocked her off her feet. Luckily, she was right near a kitchen chair. Sharon sat down and put her head between her knees, breathing deeply and waiting for the feeling to pass. As she sat there, staring down at the pile of dark wet curls at her feet, one word rose to the surface of her mind: mattress. Slowly, Sharon realized she was having a flashback; she was remembering what it had been like in the concentration camps when the women were herded into the gas chambers for haircuts. They didn't know they were sitting in a gas chamber, of course, and the barbers, who were all Jewish, were ordered under threat of death not to tell them. They convinced the women they were just making them look nice. Afterward, the women swept up their shorn hair themselves, into deep bags the barbers would carry out before the gas was turned on. Then the women's hair would be used to stuff mattresses.

All this flashed through Sharon's mind in a few seconds. It wasn't an actual memory, for she had never been in a concentration camp—she hadn't even been born until 1965—but still the feeling of déjà vu was so overwhelming that Sharon sat in her kitchen chair doubled over in a catatonic state, staring at the pile of hair in the middle of the floor without really seeing it, for a long time.

Sharon Weinstein was obsessed with the Holocaust. It had been a part of her reality ever since she read *The Diary of Anne Frank* when she was eleven years old. Sharon wasn't interested in political theories and analyses of Hitler and his death camps. To her it was very simple: in the 1930s and '40s there was a madman who hated the Jews and set out to destroy them, with the world's blessings. It was as simple as that, an old story with a new twist. The world had always hated the Jews, and it seemed to Sharon always would, though she could never quite figure out why.

What mainly interested Sharon was the literature that came out of the Holocaust, and in particular the diaries of women who had survived. As a matter of fact, she was doing her final paper for her Literature of Despair class on women who had resisted and somehow survived the camps. How had they lived through such horror? From where did their strength come? Sharon gobbled up the diaries of these women with an insatiable appetite. Books with titles like *All But My Life, And The Sun Kept Shining, Hope Is The Last To Die.*

While the books answered some of Sharon's questions, they raised a whole crop of others. Would she herself have survived? Would she have had the will to go on, after seeing her parents, her neighbors, her friends, all burnt to a crisp in Hitler's incinerators? Would she have had the stamina to work ten hours a day, standing outside in the freezing cold with nothing but rags on her feet? Would she have been able to stomach being raped by German soldiers, and would she have given them special favors for an extra crust of bread? It was too awful to think about, but think about it she did, for Sharon didn't believe it could never happen again, could never happen here, as her friends would tell her. Sharon yearned to know the answers to these questions, and at the same time she hoped she would never have to find out.

There was no logical explanation for Sharon's preoccupation with Nazi Germany. No one in her family, that she knew about anyway, was a concentration camp survivor. Both her parents had been born in New York, on the Lower East Side, children of Jews who had immigrated from Russia and Poland in the early 1900s, long before Hitler started his fascist regime. No one in Sharon's family ever mentioned the war, and their silence puzzled her, even frightened her a little bit. It was as though they wanted to pretend it had never happened at all. The closest they ever came to discussing it was last year when Sharon wanted to buy a car. Her friend Christine had a used Volkswagon Bug and was willing to let Sharon have it for five hundred dollars. When Sharon had called her father to ask about borrowing the money, his voice sounded hard and cold as he gave his final reply: "No daughter of mine will ever own a German car," he had said. And that was the end of it.

The only possible explanation, and the one Sharon herself believed, was that she was a reincarnation of one of Hitler's victims. Sharon knew Jews weren't supposed to believe in reincarnation, but she didn't worry too much about that. She worried more about why she had come back in this life, in this form, in 1985. She felt sure she had some kind of mission, but she had no idea what it was. Sometimes she fantasized that she was the reincarnation of Anne Frank herself, but mostly Sharon was convinced that she was one of the nameless six million whose bones were lying in a mass grave somewhere in Europe, who still had some earthly work to do.

After the haircut episode, Sharon became even more obsessed. She rarely went out anymore, except to go to her classes and to see movies about the war. There seemed to be a rash of them these days: *Sophie's Choice, We Were So Beloved*, and, of course, *Shoah*, the nine-and-a-half-hour documentary that interviewed Jews who had survived the camps, Polish peasants who had just looked on as the trains bound for death camps went rumbling by, and former Nazi officers, unaware that they were being filmed by cameras hidden in vans parked outside their homes. Sharon was the only person she knew who sat through the entire film three times.

Sharon's friends were beginning to worry about her. "Frankly," Abbie said to her lover Pam one night after she and Sharon had gone out for coffee together, "I get too depressed when I spend time with Sharon. She's so morbid these days, and she's always digging up some new atrocity about the Holocaust for her paper that she insists upon sharing with me. It's weird, she won't talk about anything else. It makes me nervous." Other women felt the same way, and soon Sharon was alone more and more of the time.

Besides reading books and going to the movies, Sharon combed the newspapers daily, looking for stories relating to the Holocaust. Stories about survivors reunited after forty years, stories about Nazi war criminals who were tried, but rarely convicted. One story Sharon found particularly interesting was about two Polish sisters who were hidden in a trench no bigger than a grave that some peasants had dug for them in their back yard. For three years these women didn't move, didn't speak above a whisper, didn't see the light of day. Every night the peasants would sneak out to give them water and bread, and every night the sisters would say the same thing: "Please kill us. Please let us die." Talk about despair, Sharon thought, as she studied their picture in the newspaper. They hadn't died, and when they were finally liberated, their legs were too wobbly to stand on, and their eyes were too sensitive to bear the light of day. But they had survived, and now they were journeying back to Poland to thank the family that had saved them.

And then, of course, there was Reagan's visit to Bitburg. Sharon followed that story closely: Reagan's plans to lay a wreath on the graves of the Waffen SS, Hitler's elite troops; the Jewish community's outrage and grief; and Elie Wiesel's plea for the President to change his mind and visit the graves of Hitler's victims instead. Sharon read the stories in the papers for weeks, trying hard to convince herself that the President of the United States would never align himself with Nazi Germany like that. Surely he would change his mind, and she, along with millions of others, could rest easier that the world, in 1985, was a safe place for Jews.

One night, Sharon was about to sit down to her solitary dinner of broiled chicken and a baked potato when she realized she was out of butter. A dry potato just won't do, she told herself, as she put her dinner back in the oven to keep warm. While I'm at it, maybe I'll get a little sour cream, she thought, grabbing her wallet and heading down the back stairs to the corner store. She bought a stick of butter, a pint of sour cream, and the newspaper. As she left the store, she noticed a delivery truck parked outside and a teenage boy unloading racks of fresh bread. The back of the truck was filthy, and someone had traced some graffiti in the dirt: *Doug Loves Alice* inside a heart; *Wash Me* with an exclamation mark; and all the way to the right, a jagged swastika.

Sharon stopped in her tracks and stared at the back of the truck. Maybe it wasn't true. Maybe it was an *X* or a *T*. But as she looked at it, Sharon could make no mistake about it. It was definitely a swastika. Sharon didn't know what to do. She glanced toward the store she had just come out of. The woman who worked there was always so nice to her, chatting about the weather, or this and that. It was one of those Mom and Pop shops, and the food was a little more expensive than at the supermarket, but Sharon enjoyed shopping there. It made her feel like part of the neighborhood, like she belonged. Maybe she should confront the delivery boy, or tell the woman in the store what she had seen on his truck. But then they would know she was Jewish, and then what? Who knew what someone driving around with a swastika on the back of his truck was capable of doing? Maybe her parents were right. They had always told her, *Don't make waves. Keep your mouth shut. Don't cause trouble.* So Sharon went home silently, clutching her small bag of groceries in her fist, the newspaper tucked under her arm, and a tight knot settled into her belly.

She got her dinner out of the oven and sat down at the table. Sharon opened the newspaper to study the headlines as she ate. There on the front page, staring out at her solemnly, was President Reagan, who had just placed a wreath on the graves of the SS men at Bitburg.

Sharon dropped her fork, and suddenly those same waves of nausea that had overwhelmed her the day she got her hair cut swept over her again. She raised the paper and read the article carefully, until she came to the part where the President said that the SS men were just as much victims of the Holocaust as were the Jews. That was just too much. Tears of grief and anger came to Sharon's eyes as she pushed the paper away and lay her cheek down on the cool formica table top. No, it can't be, she thought, shutting her eyes tightly, like a child who doesn't want to see what's happening in front of her and believes she can make it disappear by closing her eyes. I can't believe it. If the President can say that, can honor dead Nazis after what they've done, what will happen next? Suddenly, the image of the swastika she had seen on the back of the delivery truck flashed across Sharon's mind. Oh my God, she thought, squeezing her eyes shut even tighter. Nazis. In my own neighborhood. Right around the corner. The people I buy my food from. Now it's safe for them to come out and show the world who they really are. Jew-haters. Every last one of them. And no one cares. Even the President is one of them.

Sharon's eyes flew open, and she stared dully at her half-eaten dinner on the plate just inches from her face. It's just like Germany forty years ago, she thought, remembering the books she had read. One day you're safe, the next day they're rounding up the Jews and your next-door neighbor is turning you in. "I am not safe," Sharon said aloud, her anger and grief giving way to fear and panic. The words seemed to hang in the air, surrounding Sharon in her tiny kitchen, coming closer and closer, until she felt like she was choking. And then her thoughts became focused on the most immediate and frightening questions of all: Where can I go, she asked herself. Where can I hide? What will I do?

The next day Sharon didn't get out of bed. The phone rang several times, but she felt too paranoid to answer it. Finally, on her way to the bathroom she unplugged it, glad all the shades in the house were drawn. Even though they still let some light into the apartment, Sharon was pretty sure that no one looking in from the street could see her inside. After Sharon peed, she flushed the toilet and stood in front of it for a minute, amazed at how loud the water sounded rushing through the bowl. She remembered that Anne Frank's family had only flushed the toilet once each day, at night, and she decided she would do the same.

Sharon knew she should eat something to keep up her strength, but she also knew she'd have to ration her food wisely since she had no idea how long she'd have to remain in hiding. Last night's supper was still on the table, and there were a few more potatoes hanging in a wire basket in the corner of the kitchen, along with some spaghetti, onions, and garlic. The refrigerator and pantry shelves were pretty full, but Sharon didn't feel much like eating. She had always been the kind of person who lost her appetite when she was upset, and besides, Sharon didn't trust that her food wasn't poisoned. She knew Hitler's troops had put all kinds of things in the prisoners' food—drugs to make them sterile, chemicals to rot them from the inside out. Sharon didn't want to take any chances, especially after seeing the swastika on that delivery truck yesterday. I shouldn't even be in the kitchen during the day anyway, she reminded herself. The neighbors might hear. Sharon's kitchen was back to back with the kitchen of the apartment next door, and the walls were pretty thin. She shoved last night's dinner into the refrigerator, retreated into her bedroom which was in the middle of the apartment, and shut the door.

It was semi-dark in her bedroom. Luckily Sharon had a big box of candles in the house. Lately she had taken to lighting one a day for the six million who had died in the war. One day a few months ago, Sharon had decided she would light one candle for each Jew who had died, and it had taken her hours to figure out that it was just impossible. She figured that if she was now twenty, and she lived to be seventy, she had fifty years to do it. If she lit one candle every day, that would turn out to be 18,250 candles. Even if she lit ten candles a day, that would only be 182,500 candles, not even close to one million, let alone six. Finally, Sharon divided six million by fifty years and came up with 120,000. She divided that by 365 days, coming to the conclusion that if she lit 329 candles every day for the next fifty years, she would honor each one of the six million who had died. The numbers were so overwhelming that Sharon decided all she could do was light one candle a day and let it represent thousands of people.

Sharon lit a candle now, feeling pretty sure that no one could see its flame from the street. She felt relatively safe since her bedroom had only one tiny window that faced the building's back yard.

The next day Sharon didn't get out of bed at all until evening came. Then she drank huge gulps of water that soothed her parched throat, and used the toilet, which she was learning to need only once a day. She thought about taking a warm bath, for she was cold; even though it was early May, the apartment still felt chilly to her. But the noise of the running bath water might attract attention. So Sharon just put a wool sweater on over her pajamas and an extra blanket on her bed.

Sharon wondered how her friends were doing. It must be close to finals week, she thought. They're probably all holed up in the library studying. Sharon vaguely considered working on her papers, but school seemed so irrelevant with the Nazis right around the corner. Sharon worried about Abbie and Pam especially. She could imagine all too well what the Gestapo would do if they burst in on two Jewish lesbians, and Abbie and Pam's apartment was about as dykey as you could get, with their huge posters of naked women plastered on the walls of every room. Sharon's apartment was pretty subtle. She barely had enough money from her scholarship and student loans to pay the rent for her three tiny rooms, let alone decorate them. The one thing she did allow herself to buy were books, and she was sure to be a dead duck if the Nazis pawed through her bookcases and found all her back issues of *Common Lives/Lesbian Lives*. For a minute Sharon considered burning all her conspicuous books and magazines, but that was sure to attract attention. Maybe I should burn the whole house down, Sharon thought, staring at the box of blue-tipped matches on her dresser. Maybe in all the commotion I could get away. But then again, maybe not.

Sharon wondered about her parents who now lived in Manhattan, on the Upper West Side. They had money. They could probably get out somehow. But where would they go? And would their old hearts be able to stand leaving everything they knew and loved, to start all over again?

Sharon began having vivid dreams, sometimes at night, sometimes in the middle of the day, for she slept frequently, sometimes for a few moments, sometimes for hours at a time. One afternoon she dreamed her mother was on fire, and when Sharon threw a bucket of water over her, she dissolved into thin air, only to be replaced by thousands of yellow Jewish stars which rose toward the sky like glowing cinders from a roaring fire. Another night she dreamed she was being chased by dogs, and she awoke kicking her blankets to the floor and screaming. That dream scared her worst of all, but it wasn't the dream as much as the fact that she was making so much noise. Nothing happened, though.

And then there were the food dreams. Every time Sharon shut her eyes, images of food paraded through her mind: pizza and eggplant parmesan from Sicily's, the local Italian restaurant; sweet and sour shrimp with vegetable fried rice in little white take-out containers; moist Betty Crocker poundcake with dark chocolate frosting that her mother had made her every year for her birthday until she left home. When the war's over, Sharon thought, I'm going to eat a whole lobster dipped in butter, and after that a stuffed Cornish hen. *When the war's over* was one of Sharon's favorite ways of passing the time. When the war's over, I'm going to take three hot showers a day and eat honey cake for breakfast, she told herself. When the war's over, I'm going to get a good job and save lots of money, so I'll always be able to get out. When the war's over, when the war's over. . . .

But how will I know, Sharon often asked herself. Maybe they'll blow the sirens from the fire station, or maybe someone will drive up and down the streets yelling through a bullhorn, "The war is over! The war is over!" But how would she know whether or not to believe them? The Nazis were very clever. Sharon reminded herself how they would snatch up little Jewish children on their way home from school, bribing them with candy and carrying them through the streets, asking them where they lived. The children would lead the Nazis right to their front doors, right into the arms of their quivering parents, who would then be taken away, never to be seen or heard from again. Nothing was beneath them, Sharon knew, so how could she tell when it would be safe to venture out of her house again? But would getting caught be any worse than starving to death alone?

Sharon began losing track of time, and she no longer knew if she had been in hiding for three days, three weeks, or three years. She began having trouble telling whether she was asleep or awake. And her belly burned with hunger. Several times she wandered into the pantry, surveying the cans of Progresso soup, Bumble Bee tuna, and Heinz vegetarian baked beans. But always, as she reached for the can opener, something inside her told her to wait. Soon, the war will be over, Sharon convinced herself. And I'll be damned if I'm going to be poisoned by food from my own kitchen. She took to sucking her thumb, which grew red, withered, and raw, for sometimes in her sleep she would gnaw on it as well.

Sharon occasionally wondered why no one had come to take her away yet. All her neighbors knew she was Jewish, and a lesbian to boot, by the bumper stickers on her car. Sharon was sure they would rat on her in a minute. Especially the woman downstairs who banged on the radiator with a broom whenever Sharon played her stereo too loudly. Her next-door neighbor was a young kid into punk music and dope—he was probably too out of it to care. Her biggest concern was her landlord who lived downstairs. He could probably get into trouble himself for renting to a Jew; sooner or later he'd be sure to turn her in. Maybe he had already. Or maybe he thought she'd already been caught. He was bound to see her mail piling up. Surely he wouldn't think someone was naive enough to go into hiding in their own apartment.

Sometimes Sharon thought she was the only Jew left on the earth, and she fantasized about having babies. Babies and babies and babies until she was well into her nineties, like Sarah when she had had Isaac. Though how would she get Jewish sperm if there were no Jewish men left? Would the Nazis have enough foresight to destroy all the sperm banks in America? Maybe, and then again maybe not. Who could tell what went on in their warped minds? But Sharon didn't really believe she was the only Jew left—it was too horrible a thought. Somewhere, somehow, she knew someone else just had to be surviving.

One afternoon there was a knock at Sharon's front door. At first she didn't hear it, for she had been asleep, dreaming about lying on the beach at Cape Cod with Vivian, her exlover. They were on a blanket, naked, side by side, and the sun was so hot that Sharon's flesh was covered with tiny bubbles of sweat. She rolled over onto her belly and sighed, about to move into another dream, when the knocking on the door woke her. She pulled her knees up to her chest and listened to the pounding on the door and the pounding of her own heart, until she could no longer tell the difference between the two. Then she heard a voice call, "Sharon, are you home? It's Abbie."

Abbie! Sharon bolted up in bed. Abbie was alive! Quickly and quietly she crept out of bed and down the hallway to the front door. But just as she reached for the doorknob and was about to turn it, a cold fear surged through her body. What if it was a trick? It was Abbie, Sharon was sure of that by her voice, but what if she was working for the Nazis, helping them round up Jewish lesbians? Abbie would never do that out of her own free will, of course, but if she had been caught, would she sacrifice her own life in order to spare her friends, or would the will to live take over, pushing her to survive at any cost?

Sharon pressed her body against the door, listening for any clues that might tell her if Abbie was alone or not. It sounded like she was, but then again the Nazis could be waiting downstairs in the hallway or outside on the street. Sharon didn't know what to do.

She couldn't blame Abbie really. She had read stories about prisoners who had survived at the cost of other people's lives, people they knew and loved, even members of their own families. Who, in this type of situation, had the right to sit in judgment? She had even read an account of a Jewish nurse who had used her own personal supply of poison to kill a group of children. Later on she was considered a hero for sparing the children from weeks, months, maybe even years, of torture and suffering.

All of a sudden, Sharon heard a faint scratching noise. She wasn't sure what it was at first, but then she realized Abbie was leaving her a note on the pad she kept hanging from a string tacked to the front door. She waited until the scratching stopped, and listened to Abbie's footsteps going down the stairs, growing fainter and fainter until she heard the creak of the building's front door open and shut. Then nothing but silence.

Sharon stood by her front door for a moment and then slowly crept back to bed. There was no way she would get the note now. For all she knew, there was an SS man with a gun standing right outside her door. She would listen and wait, and if she heard nothing, she would sneak out into the hall in the middle of the night. Maybe I should wait a few days, just to be sure, Sharon thought. But then again, maybe Abbie was working for the resistance and she had to meet her soon in order to make her connection and get away. Abbie always was the political type; circulating petitions to stop the building of more MX missiles, going door to door to convince people to vote no on the antiabortion question. Her latest project was organizing a women's construction brigade to go down and help build a school in Nicaragua. Abbie would never betray me, Sharon convinced herself. I'm positive. But then again, when it comes to matters of life and death, you never can be sure.

Sharon decided to take a chance. After waiting for hours, listening carefully all the while, she got up from her bed and walked toward the door. First though, she took a hammer from her tool box in the hall closet. If there was a Nazi outside her door, it was more than likely he'd have a gun, but at least she'd go down fighting.

Slowly, Sharon turned the doorknob and pulled the door open half an inch. Then she jumped back and waited, scarcely daring to breathe. Nothing happened, so she pulled the door open a little further. Still there was no sound, except for the thunderous beating of her heart. Now the door was open enough for Sharon to stick her arm through. The air from the hallway felt cool against the skin of her hand as she reached up quickly and tore the note off the pad. Then she shut the door, and clutching the note against her chest, tiptoed back into her bedroom, where a candle was burning. Sharon crawled back into her bed, held the note up to the light, and this is what she read:

Thursday

Sharon—

Hi, I've been trying to get you for days—is your phone broken or what? Aren't you glad school is almost over? Listen, Pam and I are having a birthday party for Zelda—it's a surprise. She thinks it's just an end-of-the-semester-come-out-of-hibernation party, which it is too, I guess. We need some kind of party before everyone really buckles down for finals. Anyway, hope you can make it, you old bookworm. We haven't seen you in weeks. Tomorrow night (Friday), 8:00, our house. Sorry for such short notice, but I have been trying to call.

Love,
Abbie

Sharon read the note a couple of times, turning it over to make sure there was nothing written on the back. It was about the last thing she expected—an invitation to a birthday party? And what did Abbie mean by coming out of hibernation? Were other women hiding too? And was it safe to come out? Sharon was puzzled, but then she came up with three possibilities: 1. Abbie was organizing a meeting for women who wanted to work in the resistance; 2. Abbie was rounding up Jewish Lesbians in exchange for her own life; or 3. Abbie and everyone else were completely unaware of what was going on.

What to do, what to do? Sharon lay awake all night, turning the possibilities over and over in her mind. She didn't know what to do or who to trust anymore. Should she remain in hiding in hopes of saving only herself, or should she join her friends, either to help them in the resistance movement, or to perish at the hands of the Gestapo? And what about the remote possibility that her friends didn't even know that the Nazis were back in power? Wasn't it her moral obligation to tell them?

Sharon thought about all her friends who would be at the party: Abbie and Pam, Zelda, Christine, Susan, Deborah, Sue, Toni. She wondered if the SS would let the Gentile lesbians go. Sharon had read about gay men being tortured and killed in the camps, but in all her reading she had never come across any information about lesbians. If they did let the non-Jewish lesbians go, would they help their Jewish friends? Or would they stand by pleading ignorance and helplessness, as forty years ago the rest of the world had done?

Sharon read the note one more time. Zelda's party was at eight o'clock on Friday night, and it was now very early Friday morning. Sharon had less than twenty-four hours to decide what to do. She lay in her bed staring up at the ceiling, sometimes falling asleep, but mostly weighing out all the pros and cons in her mind. She thought about Abbie who had always been there for her: lending her money when her student loan was late in coming through, letting her crash on her couch when she was looking for an apartment, holding her through those first awful lonely nights after she and Vivian had broken up. And Sharon thought about Zelda—Zelda who was so spaced out and trippy that she never made a move without consulting her tarot deck and ouija board. Zelda would never survive a concentration camp. And Susan, how would Susan live without *Shayna,* her golden retriever who was never more than two feet from her side? And Pam. They'd make her cut off all her beautiful long red hair, of which she was so proud, and they'd probably separate her from Abbie, with whom she'd been living for almost five years now.

Suddenly Sharon missed her friends very much. She ached to see them and felt her heart tearing into little pieces inside her. Sharon held her palms up to her chest and pressed inward, as if the strength of her own hands could keep her from falling apart. She hadn't cried once since she'd gone into hiding, but now her tears fell thick and fast, as the faces of her friends flashed across her mind.

Sharon sighed deeply. What she had learned from her project about women in the Holocaust was becoming clear. It was their love for each other, their bonding, that had kept them alive. Sharon had read about a woman who traded bunks with a sixteen-year-old girl every night for almost a year, choosing to be raped by a German soldier nightly so the young girl could keep her virginity—in hopes that somewhere someone was doing the same for her daughter. Sharon had read accounts of women sharing their food with each other, food that consisted of watery soup and dry bread. Women who didn't want to die would lay down their lives for each other, just to show there was still a little bit of humanity left in the world.

And the other important thing was to live in order to tell the stories. Over and over women had written in their journals that the only thing keeping them going was a desire to tell the world what was happening so that it could never happen again. To name their suffering. To validate it. So it could be witnessed by a world deeply invested in denial.

I'll go to them, Sharon vowed, licking the salty tears at the corner of her mouth. Even if it means being tortured and killed, even if it is a trick and Abbie has betrayed us all, I've got to go. Even if only one of us lives long enough to tell the story, that will be enough. If I have to die, Sharon thought, becoming more and more convinced that she did, at least I'll die among friends, among women who love me and who will go down fighting. And then there was always the chance that they wouldn't die, that they would be organized enough to resist and escape.

When daylight came peeking through the crack between the window and the shade, Sharon remained in bed. She knew she would need all her strength that evening, so she rested. Although it was only three blocks to Abbie and Pam's house, Sharon had grown weak; even her nightly trips to the bathroom were beginning to exhaust her. As she lay in bed, Sharon thought about the things she would bring with her: all the money she had in the house, which wasn't much; the gold earrings that had belonged to her Great-Aunt Sarah, for they were 14K gold and sure to be worth something; and the silver locket her mother had given her for her sweet-sixteen. Sharon knew that whatever she took would probably be confiscated by the Nazis anyway, so it was no use even thinking about bringing the silver pocketwatch her parents had given her for her birthday last year, or the beautiful wooden candlesticks her brother made her, let alone the photographs of Vivian and herself dressed up as Vashti and Queen Esther for the annual lesbian *Purim* masquerade party, or the picture of Whiskers, the white cat she had had for the first twelve years of her life. Sharon hoped she would be able to hang onto her money, but where should she put it? Sew it into the lining of her coat? She knew eventually she would be stripped and searched and given a uniform. Hide it in her vagina? Just the thought made her cringe. Finally, Sharon decided she would keep her money and jewelry in her shoes.

When it began to get dark, Sharon got out of bed. Even though it was spring, she dressed warmly, as she had no idea where she might be sent. First she put on a T-shirt, underwear, and tights, and after that a turtleneck and a pair of woolen long johns. Then Sharon pulled on a pair of corduroy pants and two wool sweaters. Finally, she stepped into a heavy wool skirt and zipped on her winter jacket. Sharon knew how important it would be to keep her feet warm, so she put on three pairs of heavy socks. Then she wrapped her jewelry in tissue paper and tucked it in between the second and third layer of socks on her right foot. Her money went into her left boot, lying flat along the bottom under her foot. Then, exhausted from all her preparations, Sharon sat down at the edge of her bed, breathing deeply and looking around quietly at all the things she would never see again: the still life of apples and pears she had so carefully painted in seventh grade; the avocado plant she had started from a pit three years ago, now a sturdy young tree; the flowered silk kimono Vivian had given her for *Chanukah* last year.

Sharon's eyes fell on Freddie the Teddy Bear, whom she had had since second grade. Freddie was bald in a few spots, and the red sweater her mother had knit for him at Sharon's insistence was torn in a few places. Sharon held Freddie up to her chest for a minute, tempted to take him. But the thought of Freddie lying trampled in the mud with his arms and legs torn off was too horrible for her to imagine. I'd better leave him here, Sharon thought, as fresh tears rose in her eyes. Maybe somebody will find him and give him to their little girl, she thought sadly, as she tucked Freddie into her bed.

Sharon wiped her eyes with Freddie's red sleeve and then stood up. She knew it was time to go. She walked out of the bedroom, shutting the door behind her, into the living room where she said good-bye to the beautiful astrological chart Zelda had drawn for her; the picture of herself, her mother, and her grandmother they had taken in New York last year at *Pesach*; and her funky lavender couch where she and Vivian had fought and made up so many times.

Sharon stood still in her kitchen for a few minutes, mourning the clay mugs she had collected at lesbian music festivals and craft fairs over the past three years; as well as the jade plant Myrna had given her when she moved to California last year, as a symbol of their friendship which would continue to grow; and the photographs Vivian had sent her from Jerusalem the summer she lived there. Who would know what kind of life Sharon had led here, or for that matter that she had lived at all? Who would know what she had done, what she had thought and felt, whom she had loved? Sharon didn't know the answers to any of these questions. She didn't even know if she'd live through the night, for if the Nazis didn't get her, she was beginning to think her own fear would. Sharon felt cold, exhausted, dead. It was a struggle to keep moving, but keep moving she must.

Sharon walked down the hallway and stopped to get a hat out of her front closet. It's important to keep your head warm, she reminded herself, as she closed the closet door and came face to face with the hallway mirror. Sharon studied her reflection carefully. Her hair had grown in a little bit since the day Joshua had cut it. Sharon's eyes were huge in her pale, grey face, and there were dark circles under them, above her hollowed-out cheeks. Her lips were as white as her skin. Sharon stared at her reflection, fascinated by what she saw. She looked like a ghost of herself, like an anorexic teen-ager, like pictures she had seen of Jews at Dachau or Auschwitz.

She reached up with a bony finger to trace the shape of her angular cheek. For a minute she thought she saw someone behind her, peering over her right shoulder, but when she turned around to look, no one was there. Still, Sharon had the distinct feeling that someone was behind her, calling her, summoning her to action.

Tell them what they did to me, a voice seemed to be saying.

No, tell my story, another voice whispered into her ear.

No, mine, a third voice insisted.

Mine.

Mine.

Tell them how they raped me.

Tell them how they starved me.

Tell them how they took away my child.

Sharon covered her ears trying to block out the voices that were coming from deep inside her anguished soul.

"What can I do?" Sharon cried to her own reflection, and her voice sounded loud and strange, almost as if it could shatter the glass. "What can I do?" she repeated, staring into her own eyes.

Live, a voice inside her said. *Live. That's all you can do. Live and tell your own story. That's all.*

Sharon stared at her reflection for a minute longer, then pulled herself away and hurried for the front door. She knew a delay of only a few minutes could cost lives—the lives of her friends, or maybe even her own. Too many women have died already, Sharon thought, as she pulled open the door. It can't happen again, not as long as I have breath left in my body. At last Sharon knew what she had to do. Without fear or courage, she left her apartment, ready to meet her friends and her fate, and whatever else was waiting for her beyond her own front door.

Something Shiny

She couldn't believe it. But then again, it figured. Just her luck. Out of 650,000 queers standing around the Ellipse in DC, getting ready for the biggest march on Washington in history, who should be directly in front of her, with her arms around a new girlfriend no less, but Mindy, her exlover. Mindy, who only two months ago had said, *It's not that I don't love you, it's just that I need to be alone right now.* Mindy, who'd said, *I don't have the energy to be in a relationship with anyone but myself.* Mindy, who'd said, *I'm not going to get involved with anyone else for a long time. I want to be my own lover for a while.*

Yeah, right. Karen hadn't believed her for a minute. *Just call me and tell me when you get involved with someone else, O.K.? I want to hear it from you,* she'd said, that awful night of their breakup. *I'm not getting involved with anyone else,* Mindy had insisted. *I want to be involved with myself. I haven't been alone in over ten years.*

So why start now, Karen had asked, the tears raining down her cheeks. God, I was so undignified that night, she thought, shoving her hands into her pockets and trying to look cool in case Mindy happened to look her way, which was highly unlikely given the fact that she was standing behind her new lover with both arms around her waist, kissing the back of her neck. Karen looked away and then just as quickly looked back again. I told you you'd get involved right away, she thought, mentally sticking her tongue out at Mindy. I know you. I wasn't your lover for a year and three months for nothing. But somehow, in this case, being right didn't make Karen feel any better.

"Hey, Karen, want half a hot dog?" Karen turned around as Reena came up behind her waving a fat hot dog in the air.

"No thanks. You know I don't eat that shit."

Reena shrugged her shoulders. "It was all they had," she said, biting into the bun. "Hey, guess what? You'll never guess who I just saw on line at the Porto-Janes. Patty Abrams—she was my square-dancing partner in sixth grade. Only now she calls herself Sage. Can you believe how great this is? Goddess, every queer in America is here!"

"Yeah, it's completely and utterly fabulous," Karen mumbled, snapping up her jacket. The wind had picked up and was blowing right through her cotton sweater.

"All right, what's wrong?" Reena asked with her mouth full.

"Look over there," Karen said, pointing to where she had last seen Mindy through the crowd.

"Where?" Reena shaded her eyes with her right hand and followed Karen's pointed finger. "Uh-oh. Is that Mindy?"

"It sure ain't my mother."

Reena narrowed her eyes. "Who's that she's with?"

Karen shrugged. "I don't know, but it sure ain't her mother, either."

"Oh, Karen, you poor thing." Reena popped the last bite of hot dog into her mouth and opened her arms wide to Karen who gratefully climbed inside them. For a few minutes, Karen blocked out the hordes of people swarming around her, the women's salsa music blaring through the huge speakers in front of her, and the cold afternoon air. All she was aware of were Reena's strong arms and her own pain.

"Can you believe it?" Karen said, stepping back so she could look into Reena's eyes. "It's only been two months and already she's with someone else."

"It's a drag," Reena said, stroking Karen's cheek. "But this is our day. Don't let her spoil it for you. An army of exlovers cannot fail, remember?"

"Yeah, yeah, I remember. But Reen, everyone's here with their lover but me."

"I'm not."

"That doesn't count. You have a lover, she's just not here."

"I know. Poor baby, she has the flu. I'm going to buy her a present. Want to cruise the T-shirt table with me?"

"No, you go ahead."

"You sure?"

Karen nodded.

"Well, then watch my knapsack for me, O.K.?" Reena shrugged her pack off her shoulders and put it down on the ground. Karen watched her disappear into the crowd and then turned toward Mindy once more. Even though the women's salsa band was playing a fast number, Mindy and her girlfriend were dancing slowly, with their bodies pressed tightly together. When they started kissing, Karen looked away. I may be a glutton for punishment, she thought, but I've never been a masochist.

Karen sat down on the ground next to Reena's pack. All she could see from this angle were hundreds of legs—in jeans, long skirts, tights, Reeboks, Birkenstocks, sneakers and even heels. Karen felt safer sitting on the ground, almost invisible. She certainly didn't want Mindy to see her at the biggest event in gay and lesbian history without a lover. Life's so ironic, Karen thought, tearing a blade of grass out of the earth and tying it in little knots. I always thought I'd be the one with a new lover to rub in her face. It isn't fair. I'm not the one who said I wanted to be alone. She was. One of Karen's favorite fantasies was to be at a bar with her new lover, who would of course be absolutely gorgeous, slow dancing really sleazylike right in front of Mindy. Mindy would get totally jealous and finally realize what a fool she'd been to let Karen go. In fact, Karen spent much more time than she'd care to admit elaborating on the scene, imagining exactly what she would wear—a red silk blouse with a very low neckline, perhaps, or maybe her black button-down cashmere sweater. And her new lover would guide her right past Mindy, who was alone for a change, watching, as Karen's lover put her tongue deep inside Karen's mouth and her hand slipped inside the open neck of her sweater or blouse. And here was her fantasy come to life, only inside out and backward. It just wasn't fair.

Karen sighed. Someday my butch will come, she thought, leaning back and stretching. She stood up again and searched the crowd for Reena. I wish she'd come back already, Karen thought. A girl could get claustrophobic in a place like this. If she'd been with anyone but Reena, Karen would have grabbed her hand and started dancing up a storm, swaying her hips and moving her feet like nobody's business, hoping Mindy would see them and wonder. But Mindy knew Karen and Reena weren't lovers. Reena had been her best friend for years, and they had even gone out on a double-date with Reena and her butch-du-jour, as she called her latest affair. Karen sighed. I could use a butch-du-jour myself.

There were plenty of beautiful women around to look at. That was for sure. Karen turned so her back was toward Mindy and just stared. Girls, girls everywhere, as far as the eye could see. Of course there were boys, too, more boys than girls actually, but Karen's eyes just drank in the women. So many women, so little time, she thought, staring at dykes of all shapes and sizes. So many women, so little nerve is more like it, she thought, as a pretty blonde caught her eye and smiled. Karen smiled back and quickly looked down at the ground. When she looked back up the woman was gone.

When are we going to march already, Karen wondered, checking her watch. It's already three o'clock. The marchers were lined up by geographical region, and rumors were spreading that the Northeast wasn't going to march until last. Even though the march had started exactly at noon, and the streets had been filled with a steady stream of marchers since then, it could be another hour until they moved Massachusetts out. The Ellipse still looked as full of people to Karen as it did three hours ago. It's unbelievable how many queers there are, Karen thought. And what's even more amazing is the fact that so many of us gave up our three-day Columbus Day weekend to be here.

And since when has Mindy gotten so political, Karen wondered, turning around once more. This time she was relieved that Mindy and her new lover were nowhere in sight. *You go change the world,* Mindy would say, when Karen tried to get her to Boston's Gay Pride March. *I see clients on Saturday. I have to make a living.*

You think I'm made of money? Karen had asked her. *This is important.*

I'm just not political, Mindy had said, disagreeing with Karen, who thought that being a dyke was a political statement in itself.

I just love women. There's nothing political about it, Mindy had insisted. *Besides, those marches and rallies don't do any good anyway.*

So what the hell are you doing in Washington then, Karen screamed at Mindy silently. Get out of my life. She looked through the crowd again but couldn't catch sight of Mindy and her lover. Where are they? They're probably lying down in the grass fucking somewhere. Oh Goddess, Karen, she thought to herself. Don't be so crass. Memories of making love with Mindy came flooding into Karen's mind: Mindy kissing her for hours, sucking on her lips so tightly they stayed red and swollen the entire next day; Mindy opening so wide to her she could caress her with four fingers inside; Mindy taking her in the kitchen on Sunday morning, not caring that the bagels were burning in the toaster oven, and then wanting her again in the shower and then again in the living room with the *New York Times* spread all over the floor.

Karen felt herself growing wet and cursed her body for remembering. Luckily, Reena appeared at her side just then, waving a black T-shirt in front of her. "Look at this shirt, isn't it great?" she asked. There was a pink triangle on the front of it, with the words *Silence = Death* printed underneath.

"Yeah, I really like that," Karen said, as Reena bent down to unzip her knapsack and stuff the T-shirt inside.

"C'mon, let's hit the street, Kar. I'm bored." Reena pulled her pack onto her shoulders. "We can watch the marchers and then jump in when Massachusetts goes by. Hey, I almost forgot. Here." She took a Granny Smith apple out of her pocket and held it out to Karen.

"Hey, thanks. Where'd you get that?" Karen asked, taking a bite of the fruit.

"Don't ask. I practically had to sell my soul for it. You coming or what?"

"No, I think I'm going to hang out here for a while."

"O.K.," Reena said, patting Karen on the shoulder. "Karen knows best, I suppose. Don't forget our plan, O.K.?"

"Six o'clock at the Metro. I'll be there."

"O.K. See you." Reena ambled off and once again Karen found herself alone. She was just finishing her apple and wondering what to do with the core when someone tapped her on the back. Without thinking, Karen turned around.

"Hi."

"What do you want?"

Mindy took a step back as though Karen had slapped her. "I just wanted to say hello and see how you are."

"Well, I'm fine. Now you see." Karen extended her hands, palms upward, and held them out by her sides. The apple core was still in her left hand.

"C'mon, Kar." Mindy took a step closer and put her hand on Karen's arm.

"Don't 'Kar' me." Karen stepped back and shook off Mindy's hand. "Where's your new girlfriend, you know, the one you weren't going to get involved with, remember? Couldn't take being alone, could you? What was it, all of two months? What is that, a new world's record for you?"

"Karen, you don't have to be mean."

"Oh, only you get to be mean, is that it? What happened to our agreement of no double standards?"

"Karen." Mindy looked directly into Karen's eyes and spoke softly. "How's your mother?"

"Fine." Karen spat out the word. "As fine as a woman with Alzheimer's can be." She looked at the ground then, feeling tears welling up in her eyes. I hate that she knows me, Karen thought, pressing her lips tightly together. I am not going to cry. I am not going to make myself vulnerable in front of her. Not for all the queers in the world.

Karen could feel Mindy waiting for her to speak. Alright, alright, she thought, looking up and meeting Mindy's eyes. "How's your mother?"

"Not good. She has pneumonia on top of everything else."

"I'm sorry," Karen said, as Mindy's eyes filled with tears. Oh shit, is she going to cry now, Karen thought, her body tensing with anger. I am not going to comfort her. Mindy's mother had Parkinson's Disease. They had first met in a support group for lesbians with dying parents almost two years ago. Both their fathers were already dead, and when the pain got to be too much, they would joke about it. Instead of mothers-to-be, they were orphans-to-be. One night, they had even been so vulgar as to plan the big house in the country they would build with their combined inheritances. They'd have a huge bedroom with a skylight and a study for each of them and a living room with a fireplace and a big sunny kitchen. They'd even drawn the house with crayons like little kids, and then wound up sobbing and wailing for hours. It had been a real breakthrough for Karen, who was more used to keeping all her grief bottled up inside.

Mindy was watching her through moist eyes. "I still love you," she said softly, almost whispering.

"And I still hate you," Karen said, folding her arms across her chest. "I can't believe you're with someone else already, after everything you said. I knew you were lying." Karen turned her face away.

Mindy still spoke softly. "I see you're still really hurt."

"Don't play therapist with me," Karen said, her voice rising. "I'm not one of your fucking clients." Karen took a deep breath. Control, she thought to herself. Don't lose it now. "Look Mindy, I don't want your sympathy, O.K.? In fact, I don't want to have anything to do with you." She spun around and walked into the crowd, leaving Mindy alone to wipe her tears with the red bandanna she always carried in the pocket of her jeans.

Karen walked fast, elbowing her way through the crowd, not sure where she was going. She passed all kinds of gays and lesbians: dykes on bikes, gay Seventh Day Adventists, lesbian psychiatrists, a huge S/M contingent, a marching band dressed all in lavender, even a group of gay epic poets. When she finally stood still, she found herself in the middle of a group of lesbians from New Orleans. What the hell, Karen thought as they moved into the street. I always did want to go to Mardi Gras.

The crowd moved forward, and Karen moved with it, joining in the familiar chant: "Two-four-six-eight. How do you know your kids are straight?" The streets of Washington were packed with onlookers. Some were obviously dykes and fags standing on the side for support, some, tourists with heavy cameras around their necks. When they came to the inevitable Bible-thumpers, the dykes from New Orleans went wild. "Shame. Shame. Shame," they shouted, shaking their fingers at the small group of people dressed in black. Then they turned in unison, as if it had been planned, and shook their fingers at the White House, which they happened to be passing just then. "Shame. Shame. Shame," they repeated, as some on-lookers cheered.

They continued marching in silence for a while, until someone started singing: "If you're gay and you know it clap your hands." Soon the whole Southern contingent was singing, clapping their hands, stomping their feet, and shouting "Hoorah!" It was never like this at sleepaway camp, Karen thought, as they sang "If you're gay and you know it kiss your neighbor," and a beautiful woman with short grey hair turned to Karen and gave her a big kiss, right on the mouth.

Finally, Karen got to the Mall, where the rally was being held. It was already four o'clock, and she had missed a lot of the speakers she had been looking forward to hearing. But Karen didn't care that much. She felt high from marching through the streets and being surrounded by so many gay people like herself. She even forgot about her interaction with Mindy and almost didn't mind that practically every lesbian she saw was holding hands with someone. Or so it seemed. Karen wandered through the crowd, occasionally saying hi to a familiar face from home.

I'd love to bump into someone I haven't seen for a long time, Karen thought, studying the faces that passed. Everyone looked slightly familiar, like they always did when she was around a lot of dykes at a women's music festival or a political conference. Who would I really like to see, Karen asked herself, as she stood still for a minute facing the stage. Miss Berkowitz, my seventh-grade art teacher. Now there was a dyke if I ever saw one—no make-up, sensible walking shoes, pants, short hair. She'd stuck out like a sore thumb at Jackson Junior High, but all the kids had loved her. It would be wild to see her here. Who else? How about Joseph Zaretsky. God, I haven't thought about him since college. Joseph was as queer as a three dollar bill, even made it a point to wear purple every Thursday. No, I know, Karen thought, looking out again into the crowd. I want to see Charlie.

Charlie. Charlie Fineman. Karen couldn't help smiling just at the thought of him. You're a Fine Man, Charlie, she'd tease him. No, I'm looking for a Fine Man, he'd answer back. They had met in college, back in 1967, during her faghag days. My God, was it really twenty years ago? Karen shook her head in amazement. Charlie had been a flaming faggot even then. The first time she'd seen him he was wearing tight jeans with a button-down fly, only he had replaced the buttons with big rhinestones. Karen couldn't believe it. They shared a passion for anything shiny—rhinestones, sequins, glitter. They used to go to old movies together just to see what Bette Davis was wearing, and they had swooned over Doris Day's dress and matching cape in *The Man Who Knew Too Much* when she sang "Que Sera Sera," arguing for hours afterward about which of them would look better in it. Charlie loved to dress in drag, and they'd really paint the town together. Karen would never forget the night Charlie brought a whole bar to its feet when he made his entrance in a tight floor-length gold lamé gown, high heels, and a mink stole he had picked up somewhere (so P.I., but oh so sexy). Charlie was irresistible, to both men and women, though he often said to Karen, *Frankly my dear, if they don't have a wee-wee, they're just wasting my precious time.*

Good old Charlie. He always wore a tacky rhinestone poodle somewhere—pinned to his lapel or to the brim of his hat. It was his trademark. *I feel stark naked without something shiny,* he'd say, as he got dressed to go out. After college, Charlie had moved to San Francisco, of course, and Karen had moved to Boston. They'd kept in touch, had even visited back and forth across the country a few times. When Karen had finally come out, five years after they graduated, she'd sent Charlie a telegram, wanting him to be the first to know. "So what else is new?" he'd wired back. *Mazel tov. Don't start with the flannel shirts now. Remember, keep shining.* They'd kept in touch after that for a while, but then Karen had gone through her separatist phase and had cut out the men in her life altogether. The phase had passed, but so had time. Now she and Charlie were down to sending each other birthday cards, and an occasional long-distance phone call after 11:00 p.m.

I bet Charlie's here, Karen thought, shutting her eyes. Maybe I can vibe him out. She shut her eyes and repeated his name like a mantra. Charlie Fineman. Charlie Fineman. Karen had the distinct feeling Charlie was in DC. Why didn't I think of calling him? Karen opened her eyes. Maybe I should just look for the San Francisco contingent. There's probably only about 300,000 queers here from the Bay area. I should have no trouble finding him.

It was too cold to stand still for very long, so Karen started walking again. Maybe I'll run into Reena, she thought, walking away from the stage. She stopped at an information table to see what else was going on. There weren't any other events happening right then except the NAMES project, which was set up two blocks away in the middle of the Mall.

Karen had read about the NAMES project a while ago. A call had gone out for people to make quilt squares in memory of their loved ones who had died of AIDS. All the squares would be collected and become part of a huge patchwork quilt to be displayed at the march, and then go on tour to over twenty cities around the country.

Karen heard some dykes from New Jersey talking about it that morning at breakfast. She and Reena had stopped at a Friendly's, which had been completely packed with fags and dykes, and she couldn't help listening to the conversation at the next table. The women sitting there had visited the quilt earlier in the morning, at dawn, when it was first unfurled, and they had been very moved by it. One of them compared it to the time she went to *Yad VaShem*, the Holocaust memorial in Israel. Karen, who had lived in Israel one summer, perked up her ears at that and joined in the conversation. "You should definitely check out the quilt," the woman had told her. "But bring a handkerchief. It's heavy."

Karen walked down the Mall, crossed the street, and headed toward a group of people milling about. That must be it, she thought, as she approached them, for the energy at this end of the rally was different. While people were talking, eating, laughing, embracing each other, and *kvetching* about the weather in other parts of the crowd, here there was a feeling of respect, grief, awe. Karen stood still for a minute, trying to get her bearings. Not far from her, a man was sobbing loudly. People moved past Karen slowly, talking in hushed tones and walking in an orderly fashion, slowly, almost in a daze, as though they were moving underwater. Karen found an opening in the slow-moving line and took her place.

At her feet were about fifty panels of fabric, each measuring roughly three feet by six feet, all pieced together to make a big square of the patchwork quilt that was spread out attached to similar squares, covering the length of two football fields. There were hundreds and hundreds of names, so many that Karen could hardly take it in. She forced herself to stand still. Looking down, she read on a white piece of fabric, embroidered with squiggly red wool, For Uncle Frank. We Love You. The panel next to that said, For Joe N. 1954-1986. Gone from this earth, but still here in our hearts. There was a photo of Joe encased in a big red velvet heart, lovingly stitched into the fabric. Next to that was a panel that read, simply, Anonymous. It was decorated with a small, wistful-looking teddy bear.

Karen walked around the perimeter of the quilt, the thick silence around her broken occasionally by an outburst of grief. People moaned, cried, shrieked, and comforted each other. Now Karen knew what the woman in Friendly's had meant. It did feel like a war memorial, a testimony to tragedy. So many had died. So recently. And so young. Carl L. 1962-1985. Peter T. 1959-1987. Harry W. 1970-1986. Karen stared and stared. Each panel of the quilt had been made with such obvious care. They were decorated with wigs, scarves, men's underwear, dresses, photos, letters, hearts, rainbows, flowers, postcards, toys. Karen noticed a square with a big gold Jewish star sewn into it next to a *yarmulke* embroidered with the name Jacob. Next to it was a panel with two hospital gowns laid out side by side: Peter Z. 1957-1985 and Larry B. 1954-1985. They must have been lovers, Karen thought, a tear welling up in her eye.

She turned then, for she didn't want to cry, and her eye caught something shiny on a patch of the quilt a little ways ahead of her. Karen walked toward it, and as she got closer, she saw it was a rhinestone poodle. Wow, where's Charlie, she wondered, looking up at the faces around her. It's just like his. I gotta show him. Then something inside Karen froze, and she knew before she looked down again what she was about to see. Embroidered on this panel among a lavender scarf, a black sequin clutch purse, black satin pumps, and the rhinestone poodle, was the name Charlie Fineman 1947-1987. And next to his name in beautiful silver letters was the traditional Hebrew blessing *Alav Ha-Sholom*. Rest in Peace.

Karen felt her knees buckle under her as she sank to the ground. Not Charlie, her mind screamed over and over again. No. No. Not Charlie. Not *Charlie*. She reached down and touched the lavender scarf, needing something to hold onto. No, not Charlie, she mouthed, touching the smooth cloth. But that was Charlie's rhinestone poodle with the fake emerald eyes. She was sure of it. And those were definitely Charlie's shoes. She had borrowed them one evening when they'd gone out to dinner. *I'll be the butch this time*, Charlie had said, showing up in a tux with a lavender bow tie and cummerbund. Karen had stuffed the toes of his shoes with tissue paper and had almost killed herself trying to walk in them. *How the hell do you dance in these things?* she'd asked Charlie, who tsk-tsked her, tapping his fingertips together. *Beauty always had a price,* he reminded her. *Contrary to popular belief, all that glitters really is gold.*

Good old Charlie. He was always there for a laugh. And there when you needed him, too, though he didn't have much tolerance for Karen's constant moping and analyzing and existential neuroses. *It's all a comic opera,* he'd say, sweeping his hand through the air in a grand gesture. *Life's too short to be miserable. So let's be gay,* he'd say, winking and putting his arm around the nearest boy at hand.

Oh Charlie, I just can't believe you're gone, Karen thought, stroking the scarf. When did you get sick? Did it happen fast? Were you in pain? Why didn't you call me? Who made this for you? So many questions that would never be answered. I don't even have his parents' phone number, Karen thought glumly. I don't even know if he had a lover. Well, obviously someone had cared, Karen thought, studying the fine stitches that held Charlie's name in place. Someone cared very, very much.

Karen tried to get up and move on, but her legs were dead weights beneath her. Vaguely, she was aware of the line of people moving slowly behind her, stepping around her. I must be in the way, she thought, but no one asked her to move. She had no idea how long she sat there. I wish I could cry, Karen thought, unaware of the tightness in her jaw and shoulders.

All at once, Karen felt the air around her right side grow warmer. She looked up to see Mindy kneeling beside her with an are-you-all-right? look in her eyes. Karen felt her lower lip start trembling. "It's Charlie," she said, her voice shaking deep in her throat. "My friend Charlie, from college. I told you about him, remember?"

Mindy nodded. She looked at Karen silently, and after half a minute, reached out slowly and lightly touched Karen's cheek. Karen took her hand, and a second later she was crying loudly, her whole body shaking violently in Mindy's familiar arms.

"It's O.K., Karen. I'm here now," Mindy said, holding her tightly and stroking her back.

Karen couldn't answer but sobbed even louder. After a few minutes, she grew quiet, but when she tried to look up, her body started to shake and she cried again. Her grief came in waves, like the tide's ebb and flow. After a while, she turned her head to the side and rested her cheek on Mindy's shoulder. "Why'd Charlie have to die?" she whispered into Mindy's wool jacket. "Why does everyone I love have to go away?"

She wiped her nose with her jacket sleeve and looked up into Mindy's eyes. "Where's your girlfriend?" she asked, the hardness creeping back into her voice.

Mindy shrugged. "Somewhere around. I saw you sitting here, so I told her I'd meet her in an hour and came over to see what was going on with you. You looked so pale and still, like you weren't even breathing. I got scared. I still care about you, you know." She took Karen's hand. "I still really love you."

Karen sighed. "Well, I still really hate you," she said, though there was no maliciousness in her voice and she didn't take her hand away. "I don't really hate you, I guess. I just don't like you very much." Karen looked into Mindy's eyes and then looked away. "No, I'm lying. I do hate you. I hate you for leaving me and for saying you wanted to be alone because now you're not alone and I am." She stared down at the veins of Mindy's hand. "And I don't want to be," she whispered, afraid she was going to cry again.

"You don't have to be." Mindy took Karen's other hand. "We could be friends."

"Yeah. Friends." Karen said the word as if it tasted bitter in her mouth. "What good would that do?"

"Karen, come on. Life's too short to be miserable. You don't really hate me."

"That's what Charlie says," Karen said, looking up in surprise. "Used to say," she corrected herself. "I hate when someone dies and all of a sudden you have to talk about them in the past tense." Karen let out a deep breath. "I wish I had some flowers for him, or something . . . something shiny."

Mindy thought for a minute. "How about this?" She reached up and unhooked a small purple rhinestone post from her ear. "Looks like Charlie liked rhinestones."

"You still wear that?" Karen asked in surprise.

"Of course I do. Just because we're not lovers anymore doesn't mean I've forgotten about you, you know."

"Well, I stopped wearing mine the night you left. I don't even know where it is anymore," Karen said, knowing Mindy probably wouldn't believe her lie. She knew perfectly well where her purple rhinestone earring was—back in the box it had come in, in the top drawer of her dresser, where she had hidden it from Mindy for three weeks before giving her the pair for her birthday. *You wear one,* Mindy had said, after opening the gift. *Instead of rings, O.K.?* Karen hadn't taken off the earring for the next six months, but the night of the breakup, off it came. She hadn't worn it since.

"Here. Take it," Mindy said, holding out the shiny earring in the palm of her hand.

"Does this mean it doesn't mean anything to you anymore?" Karen asked, staring at the jewel in Mindy's hand.

"No, Karen. It means you mean a lot to me and I want to give something to you." Mindy rolled the earring in her left palm with the index finger of her right. "Don't you think Charlie would like it?"

"He'd adore it," Karen said, finally taking the earring from Mindy's hand. She stuck the post through the lavender scarf, tearing the material just a little, and then secured it in place with the earring-back. "There," she said, sitting back on her heels. "It almost looks like a tie tack."

"It looks good," Mindy said, her eyes taking in Charlie's panel. "Someone must have really loved him," she said, putting her arm around Karen's shoulders.

"Yeah. He was pretty lovable, alright. And some dresser. He really put the *F* in fabulous." Karen looked at Mindy and smiled. They rose then and remained standing side by side with their arms around each other. The wind blew across the field and Karen closed the top snap of her jacket.

"Are you going to be O.K.?" Mindy asked, turning Karen's collar up against the wind.

"Yeah." Karen stared at the lavender rhinestone earring pinned to Charlie's scarf. "Min, I don't want to lose you, too," she said, close to tears again. "Life's too short," she whispered, giving in and letting the tears fall.

"Want to go get some tea somewhere?" Mindy asked, brushing the hair out of Karen's eyes. "Hey, you're getting greyer," she said, touching the wiry silver hairs amid Karen's dark curls.

"I know. How about you?" Mindy looked down and Karen studied the top of her head. "Nope. Just those same three on the right."

Mindy looked up. "Come get something hot to drink."

"With you and your girlfriend?"

Mindy took her arm down from around Karen's shoulders and looked at her watch. "Well, I told her I'd meet her in an hour and it's after 5:30 already."

Karen shook her head. "I'm not ready for that yet. You go on. I want to stay here and say good-bye to Charlie."

Mindy didn't move. "Will you call me? I'd like to talk about things. See if we can be friends maybe." Mindy lifted Karen's chin with her finger and looked into her eyes. "What do you think?"

Karen tried to look away, but Mindy's gaze held her. "I don't know, Mindy. Maybe. But if *she* answers the phone, I'm hanging up."

Mindy smiled. "Well, then I'll know it's you and I'll call you back." She gave Karen a kiss on the cheek. "Have a safe trip back. I'll talk to you at home." Mindy turned to leave, but Karen reached out and touched her arm.

"Min, I'm sorry about your mother. Mine's not doing too well either."

"I'm sorry. Give her my love next time you speak to her."

"I will. And you give your mother mine." Karen took both Mindy's hands in her own. "I still hate you, you know," she said softly. "But not as much."

"Well, that's progress, I guess." Mindy looked at her watch. "I really have to go, Karen. Take care of yourself."

"You too." Karen let go of Mindy's hands and watched her walk off until she was swallowed by the crowd. She turned then and knelt down facing the patch of quilt that belonged to Charlie. Karen sat there silently, holding the lavender scarf between her two hands and letting the tears fall.

"What do you say, Charlie? Fuck the bitch, right? She didn't deserve me anyway." Karen sighed and leaned over to trace the first letter of Charlie's name. "Why does love have to hurt so much, huh Charlie? Can you tell me that? Why can't I just hate her? Why do I still care?" Karen sighed again. "I miss you, Charlie. Charlie Fineman. Nobody knows how to shine like you. Nobody. You were the star in my eye." Karen looked up at the sky for a minute, looking for something, though she didn't know what. There was nothing above her but a mass of heavy grey clouds.

"I'm gonna find a star for you, Charlie," Karen said, staring up at the clouds. "Something shiny for you. On the next clear night, I'll find you a star and make you a wish." Karen stroked the C of Charlie's name like a beloved pet cat. "I wish you peace, brother," Karen whispered. "I love you Charlie. Charlie Fineman. *Alav hasholom.*" Karen stood up and looked at Charlie's memorial for the last time. Then, head down and hands crammed in her pockets, she turned on her heel and quietly walked away.

The World To Come

Let me tell you about my lover. She is a big woman—tall, with hair the color of wheat streaming down her back in many waves. Whenever I think of her, which is often, I picture her standing in the middle of a forest, her back as straight as the trunks of the many trees surrounding her, smiling and reaching out her hand to me, her fingers spread wide in a gesture of welcome.

I met my lover many years ago, on the last night of *Chanukah*. I decided to throw a big party to bid farewell to the Festival of Lights, and I invited all the Jewish lesbians I knew.

Barbara was the first to arrive. She came all the way from California, proudly waving a collection of writings by old Jewish people that she had edited. Next to appear were Gloria and Ellen, holding hands and wearing matching buttons. Gloria's button said, I'M NOT YOUR MOTHER, and Ellen's said, MISERABLE CHILDHOOD. Deborah came with her cat Sushi, on a leash and wearing a black velvet rhinestone-studded collar. Then Lydia and Emily arrived, arguing as usual. It seems Lydia had asked Emily to bring the sour cream for the *latkes*, and Emily had brought some kind of dairy-free soy cream which Lydia kept referring to as *drek*, while Emily ranted and raved about milk products and mucus. In the middle of their carrying on, Louise walked in. I didn't know if she'd be able to make it or not, but she said she had just told her mother she was at her friend Jennifer's house. It was fine as long as she got home by eleven. Sharon showed up next, looking pale and thin, but much healthier than the last time I saw her. Karen made quite an entrance, dressed to the nines in black silky pants, a gold sequin top, and long rhinestone earrings. And Rachel arrived last, all decked out in her *yarmulke* and *tallis*.

So there we were, a bunch of nice Jewish girls gathered together to celebrate the holiday. Deborah, Gloria, and Ellen went into the kitchen and immediately started grating potatoes for the *latkes*, while Rachel and Louise sprawled on the living room floor, spinning a *draydl* and trying to figure out what the four Hebrew letters painted on the wooden toy meant. The rest of the women stood in a little group, sipping tea, gossiping about who had just broken up with whom, and admiring the new *menorah* I had just bought at the lesbian craft fair. It was made of red clay, and the base of it was shaped like a woman whose hair drifted up toward heaven, dividing itself into eight strands, each one ending in a tiny cup.

When the *latkes* were ready, we put them in the oven to stay warm and gathered in the living room to light the *menorah*. I gave each woman a candle and suggested that instead of saying the usual prayer, everyone could light a candle for the women in their hearts who couldn't be with us tonight, or who weren't free in the ways that we were. Everyone thought it was a great idea, and the room grew quiet with their concentration.

The first one to speak up was Rachel. "I light this candle for my sisters in the Soviet Union who are not free to worship as they choose." She lit the candle with a match and placed it in the highest cup of the *menorah*, to act as the *shammes*.

Gloria came forward next. "I light this candle for my sisters who have been abused. May they rediscover joy in their lives." She held her candle over Rachel's until it was lit, and then set it in the cup all the way to the left.

One by one the women lit their candles: for women in Central America and South Africa fighting for their lives; for women of Color who also live in a Diaspora; for old women, that they may know dignity and respect in their later years; for women in jails and institutions, that they may have patience and strength until they are once again free; for disabled women, that the barriers they face be shattered; for Israeli women, that they may someday know peace in their homeland; and for the women who died in pogroms, in the camps, in institutions, and on the streets—that they may never be forgotten.

I placed the *menorah* on the windowsill then, and the flames danced on their wicks and in the living room window, where their doubled reflection glowed. Everyone watched them silently, each lost in her own thoughts. After a few minutes we heard a low rumble, and Lydia placed her hands over her belly and blushed, breaking the somber mood. We all laughed. Then Deborah, Emily, and Barbara went into the kitchen to get the *latkes*, applesauce, and sour cream.

After we had eaten our fill of *latkes* and sung a few songs, it was time for the presents. I wanted to show each one of my friends how much they meant to me, and I had spent hours shopping carefully, combing the stores for just the right thing.

We all settled in a circle on the living room floor, and I handed out the gifts. Barbara received a purple pen and pencil set, and she got so excited she started writing a poem about the party then and there, on the back of her paper napkin. Ellen was thrilled with the knee pads I gave her. I had embroidered a silver labyris on one and a gold Jewish star on the other. "I'll be the best-dressed woman my karate school has ever seen," she said proudly. Deborah liked the mother/daughter book of days, edited by Tillie Olsen that I bought her, and Lydia was ecstatic over her bilingual treasury of Yiddish poetry. Emily said she loved her new macrobiotic *kosher* cookbook, even though Lydia groaned and wrinkled up her nose at it. Louise was knocked out by the book of drawings and paintings done by children in the concentration camps, and as she started flipping through it, Sharon went over to sit next to her and peer over her shoulder. Sharon was a hard one. I didn't want to get her anything depressing, but I knew it was useless to give her a present that had nothing to do with the Holocaust. Finally I decided on *Tales Of The Secret Annex* by Anne Frank, and much to my relief, she hadn't read it yet. Karen loved the lavender rhinestone bracelet I found at a flea market for her, and fastened it around her wrist immediately. "It's so fabulous being a femme," she said, extending her arm, with her hand pointed down for all of us to see. I gave Rachel two wooden candlesticks and a box of *Shabbos* candles, and when she thanked me there were tears in her eyes.

Gloria I saved for last, just to tease her, since she's told me time and time again that patience is not her forte. She opened her box and everyone oohed and aahed over the red and black lace panties and camisole set. Ellen started blushing furiously, which, of course, pleased Gloria. Then, at someone's suggestion, she disappeared into the bathroom to try her present on. She emerged looking absolutely stunning, as we all knew she would. Ellen pretended to faint, and Louise just stared and stared, and it was then that I first saw my lover.

She was standing in the doorway between the kitchen and living room, and I gasped aloud at the sight of her, as someone who is walking in the woods and suddenly comes upon a doe might gasp. She had the same kind of quiet, proud beauty, and her whole being was surrounded by a pure gold light. I wondered who she was and how she had gotten in, for the only door to my apartment was off the living room, and I certainly would have noticed if she'd come in that way. Perhaps she had materialized out of thin air.

No one else seemed to notice her. Now that all the *latkes* had been eaten and the presents opened, the party was relaxing into a typical lesbian gathering. Some women were sitting on the floor with their backs against the couch, talking quietly; Barbara and Deborah were exchanging foot massages; and Emily, Louise, and Lydia were playing charades. Louise was down on all fours imitating some kind of animal, much to the delight of Sushi, who jumped up on her back and began to purr. I knew it was time to go to my lover then, and go to her I did.

She smiled as I approached, then shifted her weight so there was room for me to stand beside her. My lover, and I thought of her as my lover even then, though she was still a stranger to me, warmed the very air around her. It reminded me of a time long ago when I had gone swimming in a cold lake high in the mountains. Every now and then I'd come upon a warm patch of water and I'd try to stay immersed in it, just as I now wanted to remain in the warmth that seemed to radiate from my lover's side.

My lover extended her hand to me, and her hand was strong and delicate, wrinkled and smooth, dark and light at the same time. At the touch of her hand, I felt filled with peace; more peace than I had ever known, more peace than I had ever dreamed was possible. We turned then to walk into the kitchen, but to my surprise, the kitchen was no longer there.

Instead we found ourselves in a big open meadow, full of lush green grass and beautiful flowers. There were soft rolling hills in the distance, and the sky above us was a perfect cloudless blue. I was still dressed in my party clothes—a lavender jumpsuit and my black cowgirl boots—but my lover, who had stood in the doorway in jeans and down vest like any dyke-about-town, was now wearing a long white gown trimmed with threads of real silver and gold. I gasped again, and my gasp made her laugh, a beautiful laugh that sounded like a thousand wind chimes all set to playing at once by a gentle spring breeze.

My lover, who still held my trembling hand, took me over to a small apple tree. We sat down under it, and a soft wind blew some lovely white apple blossoms into her hair.

"Who are you?" I asked, mesmerized by the gorgeous vision before me.

"*I am Lilith*," my lover said, "and no man shall ever own me. *I am Eve*, and I am curious and daring. *I am Sarah*, and I am filled with magic and joy, for I gave birth long after my womb had gone dry. *I am Lot's wife*, and I am filled with sorrow and longing for all that has been destroyed. *I am Ruth*, loyal friend of Naomi and humble gleaner of the fields. *I am Miriam*, and I am a Prophet who sees the truth, and everything else that needs to be seen. *I am Judith*, and I can seduce as well as murder any leader who is a threat to my people. *I am Vashti*, and I dare to defy and disobey all men, even Kings. *I am Esther*, and I am willing to give my life to save the people who are my own flesh and blood. *And I am you, Leah Golda*," my lover said, "for I am every Jewish woman who ever was, is, and will be."

I looked at her in amazement, for as she spoke each woman's name her face changed slightly, until she said my Hebrew name. And then as I stared at her it was as if I were looking into a mirror, a magic mirror that reflected back to me only the goodness that was in my soul. Self-consciously I turned from her then, and began to look around. "Where am I?" I asked, as my eyes sought my lover again, who, much to my relief, looked like herself once more.

"Why, you are in the world to come," she said. I looked around again, and what I saw filled me with such happiness that I have no words to describe it. For coming toward me from every direction were hundreds, thousands, millions of women. As they drew closer, I recognized some. There was Golda Meir, with her hair pulled back in a serious bun, and Ethel Rosenberg, wearing a simple cotton dress. I saw Anne Frank holding hands with her sister Margot, both of them with pretty bows in their hair. And there were many, many women who had been in the camps—their bodies strong, their hair all grown in, the numbers vanished from their arms. I must remember to tell Sharon, I thought to myself, as all the women drew near. They moved so gracefully, and so slowly, as if they had all the time in the world. And I suppose that they did, or perhaps the whole concept of time was irrelevant here, in the world to come. I certainly don't know how long I sat there, admiring all those beautiful Jewish women—old women and young women, fat women and thin women, women speaking Yiddish, Hebrew, Russian, Polish, Ladino, Dutch, Spanish, English, and other languages I had never heard before. But there was much laughter, and that I understood.

I would have been content to sit there and watch and listen forever, but my lover got to her feet and I rose with her. "Now it is time to dance," she said, and instantly all the women joined hands and formed a huge circle, big enough to wrap around the universe.

Then the music began, even though there were no instruments to be seen, and we started to dance. First we circled to the left, then to the right, and then we all gathered in the middle, holding our joined hands high over our heads, and then finally we backed out again, stretching the circle tight. Then the music changed, and my lover grasped both my hands, pulling me into the center of the circle. Everyone clapped for us as we whirled around, our eyes fixed on each other, our smiles radiating joy.

"*Chai b'sholom*," my lover whispered to me, and I heard nothing but her voice, even though the music still played and the women still clapped. "Keep your heart open and walk in faith, not fear. *Chai b'sholom*," she repeated. "Live in peace. Work for it, demand it, accept nothing less, so that we did not all live and die in vain." With one arm she gestured toward the huge circle of women around us. "*Chai b'sholom, chavera tova*. Live in peace." Then she released my hands and I continued to spin, listening to her voice repeating: "*Chai b'sholom*. Live in peace. Work for it, demand it, accept nothing less. *Chai b'sholom. Chai b'sholom.*" When I could hear her voice no more, I opened my eyes and there I was, back in my own living room surrounded by my friends, who had all joined hands and formed a circle, dancing the *hora* around me.

For a minute I thought I was still in the world to come, dancing with all those women, and then, as I slowly recognized the smiling faces of my friends, I realized the world to come and the world we live in are not always so different after all. I laughed aloud with pleasure, and the smiles of my friends grew even wider as they continued to sing:

Hine ma tov u'ma nayim shevat a'chyot gam yachad
Hine ma tov u'ma nayim shevat a'chyot gam yachad

How good it truly is, I thought, for sisters to gather together in peace. One by one the faces of my friends spun past me. I looked toward the doorway between the kitchen and the living room only once, and I was not at all surprised to see my lover standing there, smiling and surrounded by her golden light.

"*Chai b'sholom, eesha tova*," she said. "Sing in peace. Dance in peace. For as you sing and dance with your sisters in this world, so shall you sing and dance in the world to come."

Then she was gone. Now, many years later, she comes to me in a dream sometimes, or sometimes in a woman's face as she hurries by me on a Friday evening, a fresh loaf of *challah* or a box of *Shabbos* candles in her hands. And I think of her often when my heart starts to close up and I feel frozen with fear, or I read in the newspaper about a woman less fortunate than I am, or I hear a friend tell me about the pain in her life. It is then that I vow to live in peace, to work for peace, to make the earth a place of *sholom* for women and all other living things. For I know the world we live in can be as full of joy as that time I spent, many years ago on the last night of *Chanukah*, a guest in the world to come.

Yiddish Glossary

baruches: blessings
bat: (H) daughter of
bissel(eh): a little
borsht: beet soup
bubbe: grandmother
bubbeleh: an endearment
chai: (H) life
challah: braided egg bread used on *Shabbos* and holidays
Chanukah: Festival of Lights lasting eight days and commemorating the Maccabees' victory over the Syrians, and the rededication of the Temple at Jerusalem
Chasidim: sect of Jewish mystics founded in Poland during the eighteenth century; one large group of their descendants lives in the Williamsburg section of Brooklyn
chavera tova: (H) dear sister
cheder: traditional religious school
cholem: dream
chuppa: marriage canopy
draydl: spinning top used at *Chanukah*
drek: garbage
eesha tova: (H) dear woman
ein: one
eppes: something, for some inexplicable reason
essen in gezunt, meyn klayne kind: eat in good health, my dear child
fahmished: confused
farblondjet: mixed up
farshtunkeneh: stinking
faygeleh: homosexual
feh: ugh

fraylach: happy, joyous
futz: fuss
gefilte fish: ground fish cakes
gershray: shriek
Gottenyu: oh, dear God
Goy: Gentile, anyone who is not a Jew
hente(leh): hand (diminutive)
hora: (H) circle dance
ich hob nit ken mazel: I have no luck
kepeleh: head (diminutive)
kichel: small round soup cracker
kinder: children
kinehora: phrase used to ward off the "evil eye"
kishkas: intestines
klezmer: itinerant musicians in Eastern Europe
klutz: clumsy person
knaydlach: matzo balls
kop: head
kosher: fit to eat, according to Jewish dietary law
kreplach: dumpling
kugel: noodle pudding
kvell: take pleasure in
kvetch: complain
l'chaim: (H) to life (a toast)
Ladino: Jewish language developed by Jews in Spain, combines Spanish and Hebrew and other language of countries where Spanish Jews (Sephardim) lived
latke: potato pancake, traditionally eaten on *Chanukah*
lox: smoked salmon
mameleh: an endearment
matzo: unleavened bread
maydl: girl
mazel tov: congratulations, good luck
menorah: candleholder used on *Chanukah*
mensh: a person of character, someone you can count on
meshugeh(neh): crazy
meyn: mine
mezuzuh: (H) small oblong container holding parchment with Biblical passages, affixed to doorframe of many Jewish homes
mit: with
Mogen David: six-pointed star, Star of David
momzer: bastard

naches: proud pleasure

nosh: snack

nu: so?, well now

nudge: pushy

oy: multipurpose expression of surprise, fear, contentment, joy, pain, awe, etc.

oy vavoy: oy, and then some

oy vay: oy, and then some

Pesach: eight days of Passover, celebrating the Jews' liberation from slavery and exodus from Egypt

plotz: collapse, explode

punim: face

Purim: holiday celebrating the deliverance of the Persian Jews from massacre by the king's chief minister, Haman

putz: term of contempt, literally penis

Reb: Rabbi

Rosh Hashanah: Jewish New Year (1988/5749)

seckle: sense

seder: traditional meal eaten first two nights of *Pesach*

Shabbos: Sabbath

shadchen: professional matchmaker

shah: quiet

shammes: caretaker of the synagogue, candle on *menorah* from which others are lit

shanda: shame

shayna: beautiful

Shema: (H) most common Hebrew prayer, a declaration of faith

shep naches: reap joy

sheytl: wig worn by Orthodox Ashkenazi Jewish women after marriage

shiksa: Gentile woman (not complimentary)

shiva: seven-day mourning period

shlep: lug

shlimazl: unlucky, a loser

shmaltz: literally, rendered chicken fat; excessive sentimentality

shmate: rag

shmegeggle: (Yinglish) whiner

shmo(s): (Yinglish) euphemistic word for *shmuck(s)*, jerk(s) (obscene)

sholom: peace

shmutz: dirt

shtetl: Jewish village

shtik: characteristic way of doing something, one's act in the world

shtil: quiet

shul: synagogue
shvartze: Black person (not complimentary)
shvitz: sweat
smeckle: smile
Sukkoth: Jewish harvest holiday
tallis: prayer shawl
tanse, tansig: dance, dancing
tante: aunt
tchotchke: knickknack
töchter, tichter: daughter(s)
trink: drink
tsuris: troubles
tsvey: two
tuchus: buttocks
vay iss mir: woe is me
viffl ha zeyger?: what time is it?
vildeh chaya: wild beast
Yad VaShem: (H) holocaust memorial/museum in Israel, literally hand of God
Yahrzeit: anniversary of someone's death
yarmulke: skull cap
yekl: greenhorn
yente: busybody
Yom Kippur: Day of Atonement, solemn holiday of fasting and observance
yontif: holiday
zaftig: plump, well-rounded
zayde: grandfather
zetz: punch
zing: sing

Other titles from Firebrand Books include:

Beneath My Heart, Poetry by Janice Gould/$8.95

The Big Mama Stories by Shay Youngblood/$8.95

A Burst Of Light, Essays by Audre Lorde/$7.95

Crime Against Nature, Poetry by Minnie Bruce Pratt/$8.95

Diamonds Are A Dyke's Best Friend by Yvonne Zipter/$9.95

Dykes To Watch Out For, Cartoons by Alison Bechdel/$6.95

Exile In The Promised Land, A Memoir by Marcia Freedman/$8.95

Eye Of A Hurricane, Stories by Ruthann Robson/$8.95

The Fires Of Bride, A Novel by Ellen Galford/$8.95

A Gathering Of Spirit, A Collection by North American Indian
Women edited by Beth Brant *(Degonwadonti)*/$9.95

Getting Home Alive by Aurora Levins Morales and Rosario
Morales/$8.95

Good Enough To Eat, A Novel by Lesléa Newman/$8.95

Humid Pitch, Narrative Poetry by Cheryl Clarke/$8.95

Jewish Women's Call For Peace edited by Rita Falbel, Irena Klepfisz,
and Donna Nevel/$4.95

Jonestown & Other Madness, Poetry by Pat Parker/$7.95

Just Say Yes, A Novel by Judith McDaniel/$8.95

The Land Of Look Behind, Prose and Poetry by Michelle Cliff/$6.95

Letting In The Night, A Novel by Joan Lindau/$8.95

Living As A Lesbian, Poetry by Cheryl Clarke/$7.95

Making It, A Woman's Guide to Sex in the Age of AIDS by Cindy
Patton and Janis Kelly/$4.95

Metamorphosis, Reflections On Recovery, by Judith McDaniel/$7.95

Mohawk Trail by Beth Brant *(Degonwadonti)*/$7.95

Moll Cutpurse, A Novel by Ellen Galford/$7.95

More Dykes To Watch Out For, Cartoons by Alison Bechdel/$7.95

The Monarchs Are Flying, A Novel by Marion Foster/$8.95

Movement In Black, Poetry by Pat Parker/$8.95

My Mama's Dead Squirrel, Lesbian Essays on Southern Culture by
Mab Segrest/$8.95

New, Improved! Dykes To Watch Out For, Cartoons by Alison Bechdel
/$7.95

(continued)

The Other Sappho, A Novel by Ellen Frye/$8.95

Politics Of The Heart, A Lesbian Parenting Anthology edited by Sandra Pollack and Jeanne Vaughn/$11.95

Presenting. . .Sister NoBlues by Hattie Gossett/$8.95

A Restricted Country by Joan Nestle/$8.95

Sacred Space by Geraldine Hatch Hanon/$9.95

Sanctuary, A Journey by Judith McDaniel/$7.95

Sans Souci, And Other Stories by Dionne Brand/$8.95

Scuttlebutt, A Novel by Jana Williams/$8.95

Shoulders, A Novel by Georgia Cotrell/$8.95

Simple Songs, Stories by Vickie Sears/$8.95

The Sun Is Not Merciful, Short Stories by Anna Lee Walters/$7.95

Tender Warriors, A Novel by Rachel Guido deVries/$8.95

This Is About Incest by Margaret Randall/$7.95

The Threshing Floor, Short Stories by Barbara Burford/$7.95

Trash, Stories by Dorothy Allison/$8.95

The Women Who Hate Me, Poetry by Dorothy Allison/$8.95

Words To The Wise, A Writer's Guide to Feminist and Lesbian Periodicals & Publishers by Andrea Fleck Clardy/$4.95

Yours In Struggle, Three Feminist Perspectives on Anti-Semitism and Racism by Elly Bulkin, Minnie Bruce Pratt, and Barbara Smith /$8.95

You can buy Firebrand titles at your bookstore, or order them directly from the publisher (141 The Commons, Ithaca, New York 14850, 607-272-0000).

Please include $2.00 shipping for the first book and $.50 for each additional book.

A free catalog is available on request.